"Jethro, will you marry me?"

"What?"

For the first time since she'd met him, Celia saw she'd knocked Jethro off balance.

"Did you ask me to marry you?"

"Yes," she gulped. "I—I should have said I've got a proposal for you. A business proposal. I need a husband for three months. A temporary marriage, that's all, drawn up legally with a contract. I'd pay you, Jethro. Sixty thousand dollars.

"There are conditions to this marriage," she continued. "One of them is a high degree of privacy."

"Do tell me t

"No sex. No you'd sign a

"Charming,"

"It's a business deal—not the romance of the century."

"I get the message. No sex?" he repeated softly. "Are you sure about that?"

Although born in England, **SANDRA FIELD** has lived most of her life in Canada; she says the silence and emptiness of the North speaks to her particularly. While she enjoys traveling, and passing on her sense of a new place, she often chooses to write about the city which is now her home. Sandra says, "I write out of my experience; I have learned that love with its joys and its pains is all-important. I hope this knowledge enriches my writing, and touches a chord in you, the reader."

Books by Sandra Field

HARLEQUIN PRESENTS®
2144—THE MOTHER OF HIS CHILD

Don't miss any of our special offers. Write to us at the following address for information on our newest releases.

Harlequin Reader Service
U.S.: 3010 Walden Ave., P.O. Box 1325, Buffalo, NY 14269
Canadian: P.O. Box 609, Fort Erie, Ont. L2A 5X3

Sandra Field

CONTRACT BRIDEGROOM

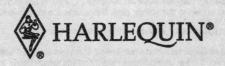

HARLEQUIN®

TORONTO • NEW YORK • LONDON
AMSTERDAM • PARIS • SYDNEY • HAMBURG
STOCKHOLM • ATHENS • TOKYO • MILAN • MADRID
PRAGUE • WARSAW • BUDAPEST • AUCKLAND

ISBN 0-373-12174-1

CONTRACT BRIDEGROOM

First North American Publication 2001.

Visit us at www.eHarlequin.com

Printed in U.S.A.

CHAPTER ONE

CELIA Scott was one hour into her regular twelve-hour shift at the Coast Guard. Her second-last shift, she thought moodily, staring out the wide windows at the sea. One more night after tonight, and she was through.

The Coast Guard offices were situated on the shores of Collings Cove, in southern Newfoundland. It was mid-September, nearly dark, the sky mottled a theatrical mix of magenta and orange. In four days she'd be gone from here. Gone home. Back to Washington and to her father.

Where was home? Here? Or with her father? Could there be any greater contrast than that between the tree-lined avenue where Ellis Scott's stone mansion stood and the narrow streets of Collings Cove?

Celia wriggled her shoulders, trying to ease the tension from them. It was time for a change. She'd been here four years, and she needed a new challenge. Something that would stretch her as, at first, this job had stretched her.

Fiercely she fought against remembering the outrageous request her father had broached just before she'd left. If she complied, she'd certainly be taking on a new challenge. But it wasn't a challenge she'd ever sought out. Or wanted.

She was, of course, totally blocking out how desperately ill her father was. She couldn't bear to think about it.

She reached for the pile of mail. But before she could open the first envelope, the security buzzer sounded. Celia glanced up at the black-and-white television screen, noticing that a four-wheel-drive Nissan was now parked in front of the building. She clicked to a view of the main door, which was always locked at night.

A man was standing by the door. A tall man, dark-haired, broad-shouldered, in jeans and a leather bomber jacket. Celia zoomed the camera in closer, noticing his rugged good looks, the stillness with which he was waiting for a response. He looked utterly self-contained. He also was quite extraordinarily attractive.

She said into the intercom, "Can I help you?"

His voice surged into the room, a voice she recognized instantly; it was the same deep baritone of the man who had radioed a distress signal a few nights ago. "My name's Jethro Lathem, skipper of *Starspray*. Would you please let me in?"

He'd phrased it as a question. But it came across as a command. "I'm sorry," she said, "no one's allowed in on the night shifts."

"Rules are made to be broken."

"Not this one, Mr. Lathem."

"You're the woman who took the Mayday call, aren't you?"

"Yes."

"I've come a long way, Miss Scott, and my time's limited. This'll only take a few minutes."

How did he know her name? "I'm here alone," Celia said crisply, "and the nearest houses are two miles down the road. The security rules are for my own good—try looking at it from my point of view."

His face was a hard mask. "What time does your shift end?"

She hesitated. "Seven tomorrow morning. But—"

"I'll be here," he said and turned on his heel.

The intercom had gone dead, leaving Celia with any

number of retorts on her tongue. Like, no thanks. Like, I'm a zombie at the end of my shift. Like, if I'm going to meet you, buddy, I need all my wits about me. Just don't ask me why.

Jethro Lathem was walking back toward his vehicle across the well-lit parking lot. In the monitor, Celia watched his long-legged stride, his smooth swing into the driver's seat. Then he drove away without a backward look.

When she'd taken the Mayday call, his voice had sounded pushed to the very limits of his endurance, yet still very much in control. She hadn't expected she'd ever see him in person: even in that brief, fraught interchange, she'd gained an impression of someone who wouldn't take easily to asking for help. Especially from a woman.

Search and Rescue had sent out a helicopter, airlifting him and his companion to the hospital in St. John's. She hadn't heard any more than that because, at the end of her shift that night, she'd caught a few hours' sleep, then flown to Washington, getting back this afternoon in time for work.

If he was a man who hated asking for help, he was also unused to having his orders disobeyed. One look at his face on the television monitor had told her that. She also knew she didn't want to meet him.

Her reaction puzzled her. So he was a macho hunk, this Jethro Lathem. So what? She could deal with hunks who wanted to invade her personal space. She was considered a beautiful woman—she knew this without any particular vanity—and lots of men in Collings Cove and elsewhere seemed to think she'd spent her entire life waiting for them to carry her off into the sunset. She rather prided herself on the adeptness with which she could defuse such expectations. So why did she feel suddenly and illogically threatened by the prospect of Jethro Lathem turning up at 7:00 a.m.?

He was only a man.

And she was quite sure he had no intention of carrying her off into the sunset. Or, more accurately, the sunrise.

The transmitter rasped out a request for the latest marine weather in the Port aux Basques area. Celia sat down in her swivel chair. Quickly she gave out the information to a fishing captain she'd spoken to many times over the years. They chatted a few minutes, Celia automatically running her eyes over the banks of equipment: computer, digital recall system, scanners and receivers. Sixty percent of her shift was spent sitting here, by herself, waiting for something to happen. It really was time for a change, she thought stoutly, as she said goodbye to the captain and reached for the first letter.

It was a note from her boss. He was pleased with her swift response to *Starspray*'s emergency call the other night, and he'd be delighted to attend her farewell staff dinner on Saturday. As she picked up the next envelope, the telephone rang. "Canadian Coast Guard, Scott speaking," she said.

There was a slight pause. "Celia Scott?"

"That's right. How can I help you?"

"My name's Dave Hornby...I was crewing for Jethro Lathem the night *Starspray* sank. I was told this is your first shift since then—so I'm calling to thank you for your part in the rescue."

His voice was pleasant, very different from Jethro Lathem's autocratic baritone. "You're welcome," Celia said.

"There's another reason I'm phoning—I didn't want you thinking Jethro was in any way to blame for what happened."

"That's really not—"

"No, let me finish...it'll be on my conscience, otherwise. You see, we'd been in port in Iceland, and a couple of days later Jethro came down with a bad case of flu; so I was on watch that night. I'm not the world's best sailor. I fell asleep at the wheel, went off course in a sudden squall and drove *Starspray* onto the rocks. Not sure Jethro'll ever forgive me for losing her—he loved that boat like she was a woman. More, probably. Anyway, I fell overboard, he rescued me, then he sent out the Mayday, manned the pumps and in the middle of it all saw that I didn't die of hypothermia. More than I deserved...I'll never live it down."

"I'm glad it all ended happily," Celia said diplomatically, wondering why she should feel so irritated that the high-and-mighty Mr. Lathem was a hero as well as a hunk.

"Jethro's one of the finest skippers around and the best of friends besides."

She made a noncommittal noise. After expressing his gratitude once again, Dave rang off. Celia put the receiver back in its cradle. She could picture the scene only too well. The elegant lines of the yacht impaled on the wind-whipped rocks of the reef; the driven spray and terrifyingly tall waves. It was something of a miracle that both men hadn't drowned. A miracle whose name was Jethro Lathem, the rangy, dark-haired man who was going to meet her after work tomorrow morning.

She always looked her worst coming off a shift. Right now she was wearing her oldest jeans, and her entire stock of makeup consisted of a stub of tangerine lipstick.

The state of her jeans or her lipstick had never bothered her when she'd been out with Paul.

Resolutely Celia marched into the kitchen connected to

her office and took a can of soup out of the cupboard. She was hungry and tired, that was all. She'd accept Jethro Lathem's thanks tomorrow morning with all the grace she had long ago learned as her father's daughter, and send him on his way. And before she knew it, she'd be in Washington, her job, *Starspray* and Paul all part of her past. As well as Mr. Macho Lathem.

The hours of darkness passed slowly. Celia ate, wrote some letters and dealt with a few routine calls. There was far too much time to think on her job, especially on the night shifts. She didn't want to dwell on her father, so ill and so intent on controlling her life to the very end. But it was impossible to keep the images at bay, or to forget that last half hour she'd spent at Fernleigh, his mansion in Washington.

Dr. Norman Kenniston, who'd been the family doctor for as long as Celia could remember, and whom her father trusted more than she did, was finally getting to the point. Celia's stomach clenched with anxiety. "Three months, Celia...no guarantees after that. Most unfortunate. Tragic. Yes, indeed." And he'd twirled the ends of his long gray moustache.

She'd known her father was ill; but not that ill. She burst out, "Isn't there anything we can do?"

"Every possible stone's been turned," Dr. Kenniston said huffily. "Do you think I'd—ah, there you are, Ellis...I was about to leave."

Ellis Scott looked keenly at his daughter's face. "Tomorrow at ten, Norman," he said, then waited until the doctor had left the room. "I see he's given you the prognosis, Celia. Just as well. No use blinding ourselves to the facts. Which brings me to something I want to say to you."

Numbly Celia sank down into the nearest chair. "I can hardly believe...there must be some sort of treatment or—"

"Apparently not. Norman called in a couple of specialists, top-notch men." Ellis eased himself into the chair across from her. "There's something I want you to do for me."

Celia bit her lip, seeing anew her father's shuttered gray eyes and rigid shoulders. Had she ever really known him? Or felt close to him? And now time was running out. Fast. "Of course, I'll do anything I can."

"I want to see you married. Before I die."

"*Married*?"

"Like your brother Cyril. Settled. Safe. Instead of gallivanting around the world taking one ridiculous job after another."

Her nails were digging into her palms. "Being a Coast Guard operator's a very responsible job."

"Utterly unsuitable for a girl."

"I'm a woman, Father. A grown woman."

"Then behave like one," Ellis snapped.

Celia took a deep breath. It would be all too easy to go down a path she'd travelled many times before; but how could she argue with her father or lose her temper when he'd been given so short a time to live? She said steadily, "I told you I'd handed in my resignation and that I'm moving back home."

Ellis overrode her as if she hadn't spoken. "You've always been foolhardy, Celia. Rash, impetuous, defiant. Time you grew up, took on the duties of an adult. Marriage. Motherhood. There must be someone you're in love with."

"There isn't," she said shortly.

"You mentioned dating a man called Paul."

"He's a friend, that's all." Paul was in love with her; but Ellis didn't need that piece of information.

"There's no one else?"

"There's Pedro. He captains a freighter on the St. Lawrence Seaway, and he'd marry me like a shot if he knew I was rich. But I've never told him. If I ever marry, I want to be loved for myself."

Darryl, the only man she'd ever gone to bed with, had wanted her money, not her. Which, at the time, had hurt quite dreadfully.

"I sometimes think you oppose me on principle," Ellis rapped.

She said with careful truth, "Right now I don't know anyone I could possibly marry, Father. That's all I'm saying."

Ellis suddenly looked exactly what he was: elderly, frail and sick. "So you're refusing my final request?"

Guilt churned in Celia's stomach, as no doubt her father had intended. Her second year in university, she and Ellis had had a terrible row, and for the next few years she hadn't seen him at all; she already felt hugely guilty for that long separation. She, tentatively, had been the one to make the first gesture of reconciliation, just two years ago. Ellis had responded with very little grace. But he had responded, and since then they had at least been in touch.

Now, however, she wanted more than that. Much more.

If only she could rein in her restless spirit. Be more like her brother, so contented with his conservative job, his country estate, his unassuming wife and obedient children. If only she could marry to please Ellis. To make his last weeks happy.

"I promise I'll think about it," she said.

Ellis said abruptly and with patent honesty, "I worry about you, Celia. It would set my mind at ease to know you were married to a good man…then I could die in peace.''

Tears flooded her eyes. ''I don't want you to die.…''

''Yes. Well. I can't control that, can I?'' He looked at his watch. ''Hadn't you better leave for the airport? That's another thing, piloting your own plane. A lot of nonsense. Far too dangerous.''

Celia took her courage in her hands. ''If my mother hadn't been killed in a car accident all those years ago, would you be saying that?''

''That's an impertinent and unwarranted remark!''

''We've got to talk about the past! We can't act as if my mother didn't exist.''

''I'll ring for Melcher to bring down your bags.''

Celia pushed back her chair. She felt like the little girl she'd once been, controlled at every turn, unheard and always a disappointment to her father in ways she could scarcely fathom. He'd never allowed her to talk about her mother. Not once. She trailed after him to the front door, where the limousine was waiting to drive her to the airport, and kissed him dutifully on the cheek.

The transmitter rasped. With a jerk, Celia came back to the present, to her office and the demands of her job. But as she spoke to a lobster fisherman about the fog patches down the bay, she found she could no longer push her dilemma to the back of her mind. Hadn't it been sitting on her chest like a lead weight ever since Ellis had mentioned the word *marriage*?

It was a dilemma she was no nearer solving now than at the front door of her father's mansion, where Ellis had offered her a chilly goodbye. She was going to have to refuse his last request—what other choice did she have?

—and thereby close another door, one that might have led to a new closeness between father and daughter.

A closeness she longed for with all her heart.

With an impatient sigh, Celia began writing up her log. At six-thirty, she washed her face, brushed her chestnut hair smooth and French-braided it. The tangerine lipstick didn't look its best with her purple sweater. Too bad, she thought, and put on a pair of earrings that she'd found in the bottom of her backpack, dangly copper earrings that, she hoped, would distract from the smudges of tiredness under her eyes.

Jethro Lathem might not turn up.

However, at ten to seven, the four-wheel-drive Nissan turned into the yard and parked in the same spot it had the night before. Thirty seconds later, Wayne, her replacement, also drove in. But at five past seven, just as Celia let herself out of the office, she saw Pedro striding down the corridor to meet her. His freighter was moored further down the bay; he must be here to say goodbye.

And goodbye it would be. No proposals of marriage from her. Smiling at Pedro, she said, "*Buenos dias.*"

Two people were coming down the stairs.

Jethro straightened. One of them was a sea captain in a smart navy-blue uniform with rather a lot of braid: a good-looking man, his head bent to hear what the woman at his side was saying.

The woman was beautiful.

She was young, her chestnut hair glowing like a beacon, her body, even in an oversized sweater, slender and lithe. She was talking animatedly to her companion.

She hadn't seen him. She wasn't even looking.

He moved back, watching as they reached the bottom of the stairs and stood, facing each other, both of them smiling. Then the man raised one of her hands to his lips, kissing it with lingering pleasure. The woman said something else that made him laugh, and then they hugged each other with the ease of long acquaintances. The man, Jethro noticed, was in no great hurry to release her.

But finally he did. With a last salute, he headed down a corridor away from the main door. For a moment the woman stood watching him go, still smiling.

So she had a lover, did Celia Scott; because Jethro was quite sure this was Celia Scott. Or perhaps the handsome sea captain was her husband. It would be a logical choice for a Coast Guard operator.

There was nothing logical about the surge of possessiveness that had rocketed through his body when the captain had kissed her hand. Just as illogical was the way he'd been unable to get the sound of her voice out of his mind, ever since he'd heard it over the radio when he'd sent the Mayday signal. A calm voice, beautifully pitched, as clear and true as a perfectly cast bell. He'd spent the first two days after the rescue in hospital in St. John's, recovering from exposure and the flu. The third day had been spent in a hotel dealing with various business matters, one of which had been a phone call to the Coast Guard station in Collings Cove to find out the name of the operator who'd taken the Mayday call and when her next shift was.

He'd asked no further questions. Out of pride? Or out of anger that she should even matter, this woman unknown to him?

A woman who was partly responsible for saving his life.

He hated being beholden to a female.

The woman he was watching so intently squared her shoulders and opened the door, stepping right into the early morning sun. Her smile fading, she blinked a little.

Her hair caught fire, gleaming in the light. Her eyes, Jethro saw, were a very dark brown, soft and warm as velvet. Her winged brows, her high cheekbones, the seductive curve of her lower lip were all part of her beauty. The rest of it was more elusive and more complex, he thought, depending on the play of expression in her face, the vividness of her emotions.

He moved forward into the sun himself and said formally, "Are you Celia Scott? I'm Jethro Lathem."

Because the sun was right in Celia's eyes, the man's body loomed larger than life, a dark silhouette that was obscurely threatening. She raised her hand to shield her vision and took refuge in an equal formality. "Yes, I'm Celia Scott. How do you do, Mr. Lathem?"

"Jethro, please," he said unsmilingly. "Why don't you join me for breakfast? I noticed a restaurant on the way out here."

Again Celia had the sense of an order framed as a request. She moved further from the door, taking a moment to assess him.

Dynamite, she thought blankly. Pure dynamite.

Six-foot-two or thereabouts. Brown hair. Although a boring word like *brown* didn't in any way do justice to thick, dark curls that had the polish of mahogany. Startlingly blue eyes, the deep, steel-blue of a sky at dusk, set in a face with the weathered tan of someone who spent a lot of time outdoors. A formidable jaw, now marred with a purpling bruise. As for his body...well, she wasn't going to go there right now. Much too early in the morning.

She said pleasantly, hoping she hadn't been gaping at him like a groupie, "No, I can't do that. I'm on duty again tonight, so I have to go home and get some sleep or else I'm dead in the water." Her smile flickered and was gone. "Sorry, bad choice of words."

"Dinner before work, then. You have to eat, surely?"

She bit her lip. "Can't we say anything that needs saying right here?"

"I'd rather not."

"Then perhaps we don't have anything to say."

"We're talking dinner at the Seaview Grill—not the Ritz."

"Don't patronize me!"

"I wasn't aware of doing so."

He'd look very much at home at the Ritz, thought Celia. "So what happens if I say no? That I've got a date with my fiancé who's six-foot-five?"

"The man you came downstairs with—is he your fiancé?"

"I don't think you came all the way from St. John's to Collings Cove to inquire about my love life, Mr. Lathem."

"I came here to thank you for saving my life," Jethro said curtly.

"You don't look very grateful."

He said tautly, "Do you have a fiancé? Six-foot-five or five-foot-eight or anywhere in between?"

"I do not. Not that it's any of your business."

"What about a husband? Or a lover?"

Celia's jaw dropped. "What on earth—look, it's nearly seven-thirty, I've been awake all night and I've had enough of this. I'm glad you and your friend Dave are alive and well, I'm sorry your boat sank and goodbye."

His lips thinned. Unwillingly, she added, "Your yacht—you loved her, didn't you?" Like a woman, isn't that what Dave had said? Women must flock round this man like gulls round a lobster boat.

"I don't really think that's any of your business."

"Then less and less do I see why you'd have the

slightest interest in taking me out for dinner," she said crossly and turned away from him.

He took her by the elbow, the tensile strength of his fingers making her suddenly wary. "I'll pick you up at five."

"You don't know where I live."

"I could always follow you home."

She said sweetly, "Are you aware that right this minute we're under surveillance? Cameras cover this entire parking lot. All I'd have to do is struggle a little, and someone would be out here. Pronto."

"All the more reason for you to behave, Miss Scott," he said, mockery gleaming in his eyes.

"Behave—huh! Do what you want me to do, that's what you mean."

"Precisely."

It was, Celia knew, the moment of choice. All she had to do was look into the camera over the door and signal for help, and this charade would be over. But she'd never been one to play it safe; her recklessness was one of the reasons behind her father's request. "I'll meet you at the Seaview Grill sharp at five," she said. "I'll have to leave there no later than twenty to seven. And if you follow me home, the deal's off."

"In that case," Jethro said with dangerous softness, "I wouldn't think of following you." He ran his eyes down her body. "Sleep well, Celia Scott."

A blush flamed her cheeks. But he didn't see it, because he'd already pivoted and was walking toward his vehicle. Standing as if she were glued to the spot, Celia watched him reverse and drive away from her, just as if she didn't exist.

What had possessed her to agree to have dinner with him? She wasn't just reckless, she was plain crazy.

CHAPTER TWO

THE alarm woke Celia at four-fifteen that afternoon. After a quick shower, she dressed in a denim skirt and leather boots, with a green silk blouse. No baggy sweaters. No frayed jeans. And plenty of blusher and mascara, she decided, making her face up with care.

Rather pleased with the result, she checked her watch and got up with an exclamation of dismay. She didn't want to start off this dinner date with an apology for being late. Not a good strategy.

At one minute to five she parked beside Jethro Lathem's green Nissan at the Seaview Grill and ran up the wooden steps. Jethro had nabbed the best table. Surprise, surprise, she thought ironically, and gave him a cool smile as he got to his feet.

He pulled out her chair and briefly she felt the brush of his hand on her shoulder as she sat down. The contact shivered through her, and it was this that decided Celia to go on the offensive. As he sat down across from her, she said, "So...are you all set to thank me very nicely for alerting Search and Rescue?"

He'd picked up the menu; she watched his nails dig into its laminated covering. "You're obviously good at your job, and I'm very grateful not to be at the bottom of the sea. So I most certainly thank you for your part in that."

"What exactly happened?"

"Oh, the usual pile-up of errors," he said tersely. "Do you want to start with a drink?"

"Not before work, thanks. When I first asked for your position, you took a long time to answer."

"Things weren't exactly normal," he grated. "What do you recommend? Is the seafood good?"

"The scallops are divine." Clearly, he was going to tell her nothing more, Celia thought, and added, "Your jaw—I presume that very impressive bruise wasn't from a barroom brawl in St. John's? Did it happen on *Starspray*?"

His lashes flickered. "Quit prying."

"Jethro," she said, aware of how much she liked the sound of his name on her lips, "you're the one who insisted we have dinner together. I hate talking about the weather—I talk about it for at least thirty percent of my shift. Dave told me you'd had the flu, that's why he was at the wheel when you went aground."

"When did he tell you that?" Jethro lashed.

"He phoned last night. He didn't want me thinking the Mayday signal was your fault."

"The skipper's always responsible. You know that as well as I do."

"He also told me you saved his life."

"He told you a great deal too much," Jethro said tightly. "Are you having the scallops?"

"You bet. With home fries and coleslaw and a big glass of Coke that's loaded with caffeine so I'll stay awake all night." She grinned at him. "So when did you bash your jaw?"

"Just before the helicopter arrived on the scene when I was so close to launching the life raft it wasn't funny. The yacht was taking on water fast, faster than I could pump."

Impulsively, Celia leaned forward, resting her fingers on his wrist. "I'm truly sorry about *Starspray*, Jethro."

It was her left hand. He said, "No rings. No fiancé and presumably no husband. Although you never did tell me about your lovers."

Lovers. In the plural. If she wasn't so angry, she might find this funny. Celia snatched her hand back. "I can see that sympathy is lost on you."

"I'm not used to failure," he snarled. "What happened out there on that reef—I blew it. Big time."

"Come off it," she said impatiently. "If you and Dave had drowned—now that's what I'd call failure."

For the first time since she'd met him, Jethro's face broke into a genuine smile. "I suppose you're right... certainly I wouldn't be around to talk about it. Do you always refuse to tell people what they want to hear, Celia Scott? Or is there something special about me?"

His smile crackled with masculine energy. "I don't have to answer either of those questions," she said weakly, and turned to the waitress. "Hi, Sally. I'll have my usual, please, along with an extra slice of lemon."

"The same, but beer instead of Coke," Jethro said.

Sally gave him a smitten grin. "Yes sir. Right away."

Once Sally was out of earshot, Celia said peevishly, "Do women always fall all over you like that?"

"If they do, you're the exception that proves the rule."

She gazed at him thoughtfully, noting the marks that exhaustion and illness had left on his face. His clothes, while casual, were top of the line, and she was quite sure the air of command he wore like a second garment wasn't due merely to skippering *Starspray*.

But there was more. A lot more. She wasn't an exception; she was no more immune to him than Sally was. Because close-up, Jethro Lathem was easily the sexiest man she'd ever laid eyes on. *Sexy* didn't begin to describe him. The curl of dark hair in the neckline of his shirt, the way the fabric of his shirt molded his shoulders, even the angle of light across his cheekbones... She found herself longing to rest her fingertips on his sculpted mouth, to trace the long curve of his lower lip and feel it warm to her skin. To lean forward and kiss him?

Cool it, Celia! You're not into sexy men. You thought Darryl was sexy, remember? And look where that got you.

Jethro, she saw with a flutter of her pulse, was watching her. Watching as intently as a hawk over long grass, waiting for the prey to reveal itself. Panic-stricken, she muttered, ''You have the advantage of me—you know how I earn my living. What do you do, Jethro?''

As though he'd read her mind, he reached over and stroked the soft line of her mouth, his finger lingering at one corner. She jerked her head back. ''Don't!''

''You wanted me to do that.''

She tossed her head, refusing to deny what was so obviously the truth. ''You've been around the block a few times—you know you don't always have to act out your impulses. Only children do that.''

''Sometimes adults do, too.''

''Not this one.''

''I could persuade you.''

The same panic was rattling round her ribcage like a terrified bird. ''Perhaps you could. Although I'm surprised you need to get your kicks that way.''

He said, as though the words were being dragged from him, ''Your voice...that night on the radio. There was something about it...I didn't really come here to thank you. I came because I had to meet you. See what you were like.''

''Oh,'' said Celia; and knew that she believed him instantly.

''Your voice is beautiful—I wondered if you sang?''

Jethro added. He was now toying with the handle of his fork, and she didn't need a degree in psychology to tell he was wishing this conversation had never started.

"I used to sing in a choir," she replied; it had been in the expensive private school her father had sent her to at the age of fourteen, from which she'd managed to get herself expelled by the age of fourteen and a half. She'd been big into rebellion as a teenager. But she'd loved to sing. She did remember that.

"Soprano," Jethro said with a twisted smile.

"That's right." Quickly she changed the subject. "You were going to tell me how you earn your living."

"Oh, I'm in the boat industry," he said vaguely, "I've always loved the sea." As Sally plunked down their drinks, he took a white envelope out of his jacket pocket. "Celia, I wanted to help you out in some way—a more tangible expression of gratitude. I don't know what your salary is—"

"I should hope not!"

"—but you could buy something with this, or take a trip... When you live in Collings Cove, the Bahamas must look pretty good in winter."

"Money," Celia said in a hostile voice.

"Yeah, money. Well, a check. You got anything against that?"

"I was just doing my job that night. For which I get well paid."

She could see the effort it took Jethro to rein in his temper. "I expect you do. I'm talking about the jam on the bread, the icing on the cake."

"I couldn't possibly take your money."

"You're being overly scrupulous," he said impatiently, passing her the envelope. "Everyone can use more money."

She took the envelope from him and tore it in half, and all the while her eyes never left his face. Then she put the two pieces on the table near his plate and picked up her glass.

"How very melodramatic," Jethro sneered.

Her nostrils flared. "You can pay for my dinner. Then we're square."

How ironic if she were to reveal to Jethro that her father was rich; added to which, at the age of twenty-five Celia had inherited her mother's trust fund. She didn't need Jethro's money, she had more than enough of her own. But she wasn't going to tell him that. Back in Washington she'd been chased too often for her money, Darryl Coates being the worst offender.

The thought of Darryl could still make her wince.

One of the blessings of Collings Cove was her anonymity. Her town house was modest and her vehicle was one she could afford on her salary. Her Cessna, bought when she'd inherited the first lump sum from her mother, was parked at the airport twenty miles from here. Her secret, shared only with Paul.

The thought of Paul could also make her wince, although not for the same reasons.

Jethro said tautly, "So how am I supposed to thank you if you won't take money?"

"That's easy. Two words. *Thank you.*"

"Words come cheap," he said with a depth of cynicism that rang all her alarm bells.

"Not to me, they don't."

"We sure don't agree on very much!"

"We don't have to," she said.

His eyes narrowed; he took another gulp of his beer. "You're not from Newfoundland, Celia, the accent's all wrong. The eastern states?"

"Washington."

"So why are you working in Canada?"

"I have dual nationality—my mother was Canadian."

"Was?"

"She died when I was five," Celia said. And overnight her life had altered irrevocably. Her father's crushing control over her had only started after he was widowed.

Something must have shown in her face. Jethro put down his beer glass and covered her hand with his own. "I'm sorry."

He'd invested the commonplace words with real force. Celia stared down at the back of his hand, feeling an absurd urge to cry. She'd learned very soon not to cry for her mother; Ellis had seen to that. She tugged her hand free of Jethro's lean fingers, with their scarred and bruised knuckles, their warmth that seared through her own skin. "It was a long time ago," she mumbled.

"Is your father still alive?"

"Yes." Just. And still trying to smother her with that confusing combination of over-protectiveness and emotional distance that had characterized their relations ever since her mother had died. For Ellis had retreated into a white-faced grief for his dead wife, grief that had been his companion for years, and that had shut Celia out as effectively as if he'd slammed a door in her face.

"You don't want to talk about him any more than I want to talk about *Starspray*."

With a wry grin, she said, "There's always the weather. A ridge of high pressure is moving into the area. Visibility excellent, southerlies decreasing to ten knots."

"Back off—that's what you're saying."

"Hey, you're quick."

Anger glinted in his steely eyes. "You sure know how to get under my skin, Celia Scott."

"I'd be willing to bet a night's pay you're used to women who bend over backwards to agree with every word you say."

"And who'd take money from me any chance they got."

Again there was real cynicism in his tone. She said lightly, "Kind of drastic that you just about had to drown yourself to meet someone who won't let you go past $11.95 for a plate of scallops."

"You're forgetting the Coke."

Celia laughed outright. "And the tip." Her brow furrowed. "What's the matter?"

He said roughly, "You're so goddammed beautiful when you laugh."

A blush scorched her cheeks, and for a moment that felt as long as an hour, Celia could think of absolutely nothing to say. Then she sputtered, "I'll make you a deal, Jethro. You talk to me about Iceland and I'll talk to you about Newfoundland. We'll omit any mention of gratitude, fathers, lovers and money. Okay?"

"Why aren't you married?"

"Because I don't want to get married!…Oh thanks, Sally, that looks great, and you remembered the extra lemon," Celia babbled.

"Can I get you anything else?" Sally asked, eyeing Celia's scarlet cheeks with interest.

"That's fine, thanks," Jethro said, with a note in his voice that sent Sally scurrying back to the kitchen. Then he said flatly, "That sea captain—he's your lover, right?"

"Pedro? Oodles of charm waiting for the right heiress to come along. Pedro and I are friends, Jethro. Friends."

"Friendship's impossible between a man and a woman."

"I disagree!"

"Do you mean to say you never got into his bed?" he grated. "Or should I say his bunk?"

"That's precisely what I'm saying," Celia announced and ferociously stabbed a scallop onto her fork.

Jethro leaned back in his chair. "Don't take it out on your dinner, Celia. Tell me to get lost."

"I'm going to finish eating first. I've got a twelve-hour shift ahead of me, or are you forgetting that?"

"Friend," he repeated in an unreadable voice.

"That's what I said. Why do you find it so hard to believe?"

"Oh, that's a long story and not one I'm about to tell. So why don't we talk about Iceland instead? We were only there three days—just long enough for me to contract the flu. But while we were there, a friend of Dave's drove us to the Hekla volcano."

As he kept talking, Celia ate another scallop, willing the color to fade from her cheeks. But Jethro was both entertaining and informed, and soon she forgot her self-consciousness, asking questions, telling him about her trip up the Labrador coast on the freight boat, and some of her adventures in scallop draggers offshore. Sally brought two pieces of chocolate cream pie, followed by coffee. Celia was leaning forward laughing at something Jethro had said, when he remarked, "I think that man wants to talk to you."

Celia glanced up; her smile vanished as if it had been wiped from her face. "Paul..." she faltered.

Dr. Paul Fielding ran the clinic in Collings Cove. He was pleasant-faced, hard-working, and head over heels in love with her. She'd done nothing to encourage him, even while wondering why she didn't—couldn't—fall in love with him. He was everything Darryl wasn't, he'd be un-failingly good to her, and he didn't care about her money.

But she'd never felt impelled into his bed. He'd have been willing; she was the one with the problem.

"Paul," she said, "this is Jethro Lathem. You remember I told you about the Mayday call last week? It was Jethro's boat."

"How do you do?" Paul said, without any real warmth.

"Why don't you join us for coffee?" Jethro said smoothly.

Sally was hovering in the background, as bright-eyed as if her favorite soap opera was playing. "Want a piece of pie to go with your coffee, doc?"

"Just the coffee, Sally, thanks." Paul switched his attention to Celia. "All set for the dinner on Saturday? Six-thirty, isn't it?"

He was, with no subtlety whatsoever, laying claim to her. Why couldn't she have fallen in love with him? If she'd accepted the heirloom ring he'd kept pressing on her, it would have made her father happy. She'd be married. Settled in Collings Cove for the rest of her life, and what could be safer than that? "Six-thirty for seven," she said, and started describing the clinic to Jethro. She didn't want Jethro knowing it was a farewell dinner.

Sally brought the coffee in record time. Her blond curls bobbing, she said, "Celia, you make sure you come back here before you head to Washington. I'll see you get a piece of pie on the house, you betcha."

"You're leaving here?" Jethro demanded.

"Tonight's her last shift," Paul said glumly.

"You didn't tell me that," Jethro said.

"Why should I?" Celia responded in open defiance. She glanced at her watch. "Talking of shifts, I'll have to go in five minutes."

Sally brought the bill, Jethro paid, and all three of them

got up. As Celia walked past the cash register, Sally winked at her. "Have a good evening."

"I'm going to work," Celia said repressively, stomped down the steps and marched toward her car, Paul hot on her heels. As she unlocked the door, he grabbed her in his arms, planted a clumsy kiss in the vicinity of her mouth and said loudly, "I'll call you tomorrow."

With a brief nod at Jethro, he climbed into his battered Jeep and drove off, gravel spitting from his tires. Jethro said, "Why don't you marry him and put him out of his misery? The man's besotted with you."

"I know you must find this difficult to believe—most men do—but I don't want to marry anyone!"

"I could better that kiss."

The keys dropped from her hand. The evening sun gilded Jethro's dark hair, the breadth of his shoulders in his leather jacket, his flat belly under his denim shirt. He was three or four inches taller than Paul; he possessed in spades what Paul lacked. Sex appeal. Charisma. Animal magnetism.

And didn't he know it!

She picked up her keys, swung into her seat and slammed the door. "You're not going to get the chance to try. Thanks for dinner. You can write me off the books—you don't owe me a red cent."

He was rocking back and forth on the balls of his feet. "I'll decide what I do or don't owe you, Celia."

If only he wasn't so devastatingly attractive. If only he didn't make her blood thrum in her veins and all her recklessness leap to the fore. As she turned the key in the ignition, she found herself gazing at him as though she wanted to imprint him on her memory; because, of course, she wouldn't be seeing him again. "Goodbye, Jethro," she said, and suddenly gave him a wicked grin. "You've left Sally with enough gossip for the next week. Not bad for one scallop dinner.''

"Then maybe I'll have to eat there again.''

She didn't want him staying in Collings Cove. She wanted him gone. Out of her life. She said coolly, "Stay away from the steak, it's as tough as your hide.''

Unexpectedly he began to laugh. The way his eyes crinkled at the corners made her want to salivate. Get me out of here, Celia thought wildly.

She jammed the Toyota into reverse, swung round and drove away as fast as she could.

Jethro watched Celia drive off. Then he went back to his motel, where he phoned the airport, discovering there was a flight out early in the morning. "I'll call you in five minutes to confirm,'' he said.

Going straight to the top drawer of the bureau, he unfolded the weekly issue of the local paper that was stashed there. It had come out two days after *Starspray* had sunk. Quickly he ran his eyes down the column. The journalist had done her homework. The article referred to Jethro as an international financier, owner of a huge fleet of oil tankers and container ships. Filthy rich, in other words.

Celia would have seen the paper. In a place this size, she couldn't have avoided it. So, was her refusal to take any money from him genuine? Or merely a clever ploy?

She was highly intelligent. It was one of the several reasons he was so attracted to her. Intelligent enough to play a double game? He was rich beyond anything Collings Cove could imagine. Was there a woman born who could turn her nose up at his money? More to the point, was Celia Scott that woman?

Did he want to hang around long enough to find the answer?

He'd never chased a woman in his life. Never had to. And anyone who was as prickly as Celia, he dropped quicker than a plugged nickel. Why bother with a female who wasn't going to come across when the world was full of those who would?

Anyway, he'd known a lot of women more classically beautiful than Celia. Certainly more sophisticated. She wasn't his type.

So why was he so intrigued by the way her flame-filled hair contrasted with the dark pools of her eyes? How temper painted a flush over her cheekbones and the hollows beneath them? The delicious curve of her mouth when she laughed?

She laughed as though she meant it. Yet her dead mother still caused her sorrow.

Dammit, man, will you forget Celia Scott? You're going to go back to Manhattan tomorrow morning and start planning your next challenge. After all, isn't your whole life organized around challenging yourself? You can't do any more solo races in *Starspray*. But those peaks in the Andes in Peru, you could take an expedition down there in the next six months....

Impatiently Jethro reached for the phone.

A gray jay squawked from the trees. The breeze smelled pungently of resin and peat, and impetuously Celia pulled off the elastic holding her ponytail and shook out her hair for the wind to play with. A seagull swooped overhead, pristinely white. Free, she thought. Free.

She'd broken her own record. Normally it took her an hour and a quarter to climb Gun Hill, the small mountain behind Collings Cove. But this afternoon she'd done it in sixty-five minutes.

Because she didn't want to think about Jethro, who

must have left town this morning on the early flight? She sure didn't want to think about the dream she'd had, in which they'd both been stark naked in a bunk on a scallop dragger.

Or was her headlong rush up the hill to keep at bay the dilemma of her father, who wanted her married and settled and safe. What was she going to do about his request?

What could she do?

Nothing.

Celia sighed. She was glad she was going back to Washington. Even if she couldn't get married to please Ellis, she could at least spend these last few months with him. And who knows, maybe they'd be able to bridge the gap that had widened so drastically with the years. She'd like that. She'd like it very much—enough to put all her energy and imagination into bringing it about.

She sat down on the wind-scoured rocks of the peak and took out an apple, chewing with keen pleasure, then tossing the core to a passing raven.

Behind her she heard a scrape on the rocks.

The hair rose on the back of her neck. She stood up. Picking each step so as not to make a sound, she crossed the rocks to the crest of the north face. Even though logic was telling her it was an unlikely place to find a wild animal, a rattle of falling stones came to her ears. A bear? And her face-to-face with it? Holding her breath, she peered over the edge.

A man was climbing the last few yards of the northern escarpment, every movement smooth and economical. Jethro.

He hadn't left on the morning plane.

Her first reaction was sheer joy, her second dismay. She had no desire to come face-to-face with him, either, she thought, stifling that treacherous—and meaningless—

surge of pleasure. Swiftly, before he could look up, she retreated from the edge. But there was nowhere to hide, and even if she scuttled back down the trail, Jethro would see her: the treeline was well down the slope. Is that what she wanted? To be found in retreat, scurrying for shelter like a frightened rabbit? No way.

So Celia stood her ground, and as Jethro's crop of dark hair appeared over the crest of rock, she said cordially, "Good afternoon, Jethro."

His body froze to utter stillness, his fingernails digging into the rock. He hadn't known she was here: that was obvious. He must have parked on the north side of Gun Hill, where he wouldn't have seen her car.

In a single lithe movement he hauled himself onto the peak: he wasn't even breathing hard. Standing up, he rubbed the dirt from his fingers down the sides of his shorts. "Celia."

She had no idea what he was thinking; inscrutability had been invented with him in mind. Of its own accord, her gaze fell lower, to his long, strongly muscled legs. In her dream, they'd wrapped themselves around her thighs, molding her to his body. She blurted, "I came up here to be alone."

"So, oddly enough, did I."

"I'll leave then, I have to go home and get ready for the movers, they're coming first thing in the morning and—"

Jethro took two steps toward her, put his arms around her and kissed her.

CHAPTER THREE

FOR A FULL two seconds Celia stood rigid with shock, too startled to struggle. Then the firm pressure of Jethro's lips, the warmth of his skin, the sureness with which he was coaxing her lips apart, flooded her with a wild, sweet pleasure that rippled through her limbs as inexorably as the tides rose on the beach. Sheer heaven, Celia thought, and kissed him back, her body pliant in his embrace, her hands sliding up his chest to circle his nape.

He was the heat of the sun and the freedom of the wind: everything that was elemental. He was her dream, flowering into reality in her body.

Then Jethro strained her toward him, pulling her the length of his frame, one hand burying itself in her hair, the other moving from her waist to clasp the swell of her hip.

He was fully aroused. Desire was like a sunburst in her belly, aflame with hunger and golden with pleasure, to which she surrendered with a low moan of delight. As Jethro thrust with his tongue, the flames leapt higher, encompassing her in their implacable demands. She felt his hands sweep the curve of her spine, drawing her still closer, heard him mutter her name against her lips. Her nostrils filled with the male scent of a man she had expected never to see again.

Briefly he loosened his hold, his hands reaching for the hem of her sweatshirt. Her breath caught in her throat as desire was suddenly eclipsed by terror. Darryl had done the same thing. Kissed her, then tried to fondle her breasts. But Darryl hadn't listened when she'd asked him to stop.

She pulled back with an inarticulate cry. "Don't, Jethro! Please, don't."

Her palms were flat against his chest; he was wearing a T-shirt that was like a second skin, through which she could feel the taut curve of his ribs and the heavy pounding of his heart. He said tersely, "What's wrong?"

"Everything! We shouldn't be doing this, it's crazy—"

"Don't try and tell me you didn't like it—I know better."

"Maybe I did like it. But not any more."

Very deliberately he released her, stepping back, his face like a carved mask; the bruise on his jaw stood out like a brand. "Why not?"

"We don't even know each other, we—"

"I'd say we found out one hell of a lot about each other in that kiss."

"I'm leaving here on Sunday and we'll never see each other again—what are you looking for, a quick lay?"

His jaw tightened. "Why were you up here waiting for me, then?"

"Waiting for you?" she squawked, almost inarticulate with rage. "You think I was *waiting* for you?"

"You must have known I was coming up here—I don't believe in coincidence."

"Then you'd better expand your horizons. I most certainly didn't know you were up here or I'd have stayed away. I told you, I wanted to be alone."

"Come off it—you saw my Nissan parked down below and you climbed the south slope because it's quicker."

If she had any sense, she'd run straight back down the south slope: Jethro looked angry enough to be a greater threat than any bear. "I've got better things to do than chase men up mountains,'' Celia blazed. "I said goodbye to you last night and I meant it. I don't play games and I sure didn't climb all the way up here just to have a fight with you.''

"So what was wrong with that kiss, Celia? Because that's all it was—a kiss. You think I was about to make love to you on top of a chunk of solid rock? I'm not that desperate.''

"Aren't you? You were giving a damn good imitation!''

"Do I have to spell it out for you?'' he sneered. "You're beautiful and sexy and it's been a long time since I've bedded anyone. A very long time. Get the picture?''

"I sure do. You have a real way with compliments— that kiss was nothing to do with me, any female would have done.''

"It had everything to do with you!''

"Oh yeah?''

"Oh yeah.'' He raked his fingers through his hair. "Why did you get so frightened?''

Her temper died. He'd just asked the sixty-four-thousand-dollar question, the one that led her straight back to Darryl. But her heart was no longer trying to batter its way out of her ribcage and Jethro had, after all, let her go when she'd asked him to. Perhaps she owed him the truth. She said, choosing her words, "I had a bad experience with a man once, and I don't want to repeat it.'' From somewhere she dredged up a smile. "The way I backed off—don't take it personally, in other words.''

His face had hardened. "Were you raped?''

"No. A friend turned up at the door so he stopped.''

"Son of a bitch,'' Jethro said in a ugly voice.

Her tension collapsed in a smile. "For once, we're in agreement.''

"How long ago did it happen?"

"Four or five years ago."

"You've gone to bed with the doctor since then."

She tossed her wind-tangled curls. "I have not."

"You're not telling me you're a virgin?" Jethro said incredulously. "I don't believe you."

"Imagine that," Celia said nastily. "Jethro, this has been all very entertaining, but I have to go home. I've got a ton of things to do."

He looked like a man doing some hard thinking. "We can walk down together."

"Your vehicle's parked in the north lot."

"If I can climb K2, I'm sure I can walk as far as my car."

"K2?" she repeated, and wondered why she wasn't surprised. K2 was probably the most difficult mountain in the world, a much more demanding climb than Everest. No wonder Jethro hadn't been breathing hard at the top of Gun Hill.

He gave an exasperated sigh. "Back home, I have a reputation for being close-mouthed—that's a laugh."

Celia said evenly, "Why didn't you fly out this morning?"

"Wasn't ready to."

"You had this sudden, irresistible urge to climb Gun Hill," she said sarcastically.

He raised his brow. "One thing I like about you is your intelligence."

It was on the tip of her tongue to ask what else he liked. The way she'd kissed him as if there were no tomorrow? As if they were standing on top of the world, responsible to no one? "Let's go," she said stiffly. "I shouldn't even have come up here—my cupboards are a disaster and the movers arrive first thing in the morning."

She started down the hill ahead of him, picking her way through the boulders and pockets of soggy peat to the treeline, where rusty-tipped ferns brushed her knees. And with every step she took, she was trying to banish the memory of a kiss that had turned her world upside down. She'd never felt even remotely like that when Paul had kissed her; which must be the reason she'd stayed out of his bed.

A flock of kinglets peeped in the trees; shadows slanted across her path. Then Jethro touched her shoulder from behind. "Look, Celia, an eagle."

Shading her eyes with her hand, Celia watched the great brown wings circle the thermals, the sun dazzling on the bird's white head and outspread tail. "Wonderful," she murmured. "Look how it soars...now that's freedom."

His dark blue eyes resting on her face, Jethro said, "Freedom...is that why you haven't married?"

Married. Her father. Jethro.

The words fell together like the last pieces of a very complicated jigsaw puzzle. Without stopping to think, Celia gasped, "Jethro, are you married?"

"Nope."

"Engaged? Living with someone? Otherwise spoken for?"

"No, no and no. What are you getting at, Celia?"

She gaped at him. "N-nothing, I was just curious," she stammered, turned on her heel and started down the path as though ten black bears were after her.

She couldn't. She'd be out of her mind.

Ask Jethro Lathem to marry her? A man compounded of sex appeal, rage and mystery? A man who had only to kiss her to make her understand, truly understand for the first time in her life, the meaning of desire?

Get a life, Celia.

But who else could she ask?

Forcing herself to concentrate on the rough trail, skidding on stones, Celia leaped from rock to rock with the agility of panic. She wouldn't ask Paul to take on a fake marriage, he'd be horribly hurt. Nor could she ask Darryl or Pedro, either of whom would be delighted. Or any of the men back in Washington who'd been more interested in her father's fortune than in her.

Jethro didn't know about her money. And there was no way she could hurt him; she knew instinctively that he'd never let her close enough to do that.

She couldn't ask him. She couldn't.

Out of the question.

A spruce bough slapped Celia's cheek. Her heart was racing in her breast in a way that had nothing to do with her precipitous descent of Gun Hill. She'd never been a coward before. Was she going to start now? Her father could be dead in three months, any chance of reconciliation gone. Is that what she wanted?

How far was she willing to go to set Ellis Scott's mind to rest in the short time he had left? A long way, she thought. A very long way. Deep down she was still bitterly ashamed of their last horrific argument. At the age of nineteen, in her second year at Harvard, she'd discovered that her father had been having her watched; she was being followed by a bodyguard he'd hired. And she'd lost it.

She'd taken the first train home and confronted Ellis, and as though a lock had broken on her tongue, the pent-up feelings of years had poured out: her loneliness in those bleak months after her mother's death, when her father had retreated from her in all the ways that mattered. Her resentment of his unceasing control of her actions, the nannies who'd forbidden her to climb trees, the directives to the schools banning her from the high-diving towers and the gymnastic equipment. Her fury when he'd refused to sponsor her for the junior slalom team when she was fourteen; too dangerous, he'd said.

Control, control, control.

She'd yelled at him, her fists clenched at her sides, tears streaming down her face. He hadn't yelled back. She'd have preferred it if he had. In a cold, clipped voice he'd accused her of ingratitude and wanton rebellion; she was anything, he'd said, but her mother's daughter. Which had been the unkindest cut of all.

He'd been cruel, certainly, that day eight years ago. But was that how she wanted to remember him?

It was all too easy to interpret his wish to see her married as yet another strand in that stifling overprotectiveness, as one more link in those manacles of control. Older now, perhaps a little wiser, Celia was finally prepared to consider the possibility that this was the only way Ellis knew how to say he loved her.

She loved him, too. Of course she did. Although it was a very long time since she'd told him so.

She could stand anything for three months, surely? Even a fake marriage whose sole intent was to relieve her father of a burden of anxiety he'd carried for years.

She bit her lip. Do it, Celia. Do it. Now.

Because there's nobody else to ask. And you'll regret it for the rest of your life if you don't make peace with your father.

She stopped dead in her tracks. Jethro cannoned into her, his arms going round her in a reflex action, circling her waist. She twisted in his embrace and said with the bluntness of desperation, ''Jethro, will you marry me?''

''*What*?''

For the first time since she'd met him, Celia saw she'd knocked Jethro off balance. He'd paled under his tan; his eyes were like twin blades of steel. She bit her lip. "Oh God, that's not what I meant to say. At least, it is, but not—"

"Did you ask me to *marry* you?"

"Yes," she gulped. "But it's not what you think, it's—"

"You don't have any idea what I'm thinking," he said with menacing softness. "Nor do you want to know."

"I-I should have said I've got a proposal for you. A business proposal."

"You're just like the rest of them."

His voice was as caustic as acid. "What do you mean?" she blurted.

"For a while I thought...but I should have known better. You saw the newspaper article, didn't you, Celia? Of course you did. Although I'll give you this—your tactics are different than most."

"I don't have any idea what—"

"Oh, for God's sake!" he exploded. "Quit pretending, will you? The game's over."

"If you'd keep quiet for a minute and listen, I'll tell you what I'm—"

"The voice of an angel and a beauty that knocks me sideways—I thought I was too old to fall for that crap."

"Jethro," Celia said tautly, "stop looking at me like I'm some kind of disgusting squishy thing you've turned up under a rock. My proposal's strictly business—do you hear me?"

Her voice had risen. "Yeah," he drawled, "I hear you."

She was still standing locked in his embrace, her palms flat to his T-shirt. He smelled faintly of sweat; he looked thoroughly dangerous and not at all business-like. The trouble was, she didn't feel business-like, either. Not with his mouth only inches from hers, his lean, hard body pressed against hers. She said frantically, "Strictly business," and struggled to keep her wits. "I need a husband for three months. A temporary marriage, that's all, drawn up legally with a contract."

"That's all?" he repeated, with a depth of sarcasm that made her flinch.

"I'd pay you, Jethro. Quite a lot of money. You'd be able to put it toward another boat to replace *Starspray*."

"You let me worry about *Starspray*," he snarled. "You don't know the first thing about me and you're asking me to marry you? I take back what I said about your intelligence. You're out to lunch, lady."

Every nerve pulled tight, Celia gazed up at him. Beneath a formidable level of rage, he looked...was disappointed the right word? Ferociously disappointed, as though somehow she'd let him down. In a major way. She said defiantly, "I know quite a lot about you. You're courageous—you rescued your friend, didn't you? You're an adventurer, with the guts and determination to climb the most challenging mountain in the world. You've got class. Tons of it. And up there on the mountain top when I said no, you backed off." Suddenly she pushed away from him. "I'm doing this all wrong!"

"You finally got something right. Why three months, Celia? And where are you going to get the money to pay me? Rob a bank?"

The wind wafted a long strand of hair across her face. She pushed it back and said steadily, "My father's a rich man. And two years ago I inherited my mother's trust fund. Sixty thousand dollars, that's what I'm prepared to pay you."

The amount she named didn't even make him blink. He pounced with the speed of a predator. "So why are you working for the Coast Guard if you've got that much money?"

"There are conditions to this marriage," she said flatly. "One of which is a high degree of privacy."

"Do tell me the others."

She hated that note in his voice; it made her feel about ten years old. "No sex. No contact after the time's up—you'd vanish from my life and you wouldn't come back. Ever. And you'd sign a contract to that effect."

"Charming," Jethro said.

"It's a business deal—I told you that! Not the romance of the century."

"I get the message—I'm not totally devoid of brains. Although I must admit when I offered to help you as a way of thanking you for saving my life, marriage wasn't what I had in mind." He picked up a handful of her hair, running it through his fingers; in the afternoon sun it glinted like the most delicate copper wire. "No sex?" he repeated softly. "Are you sure about that?"

She pulled back, feeling the tug at her scalp, panic nibbling at her control. "No sex. That's what I said."

His hands dropped to his sides. "The answer's no."

"But—"

"I don't give a damn how rich you are, I'm not into being bought."

He meant it. The contempt in his face seemed to strip Celia naked, leaving her utterly defenceless and deeply ashamed. He loathed her, she thought numbly. Despised her for trying to buy him as though he were a stick of furniture. Oh God, why had she started this?

With a tiny whimper of distress, she whirled and ran down the slope, tears blurring her vision. What a fool

she'd been! Why hadn't she stopped to think? Isn't that
what had so often angered her father, that she acted before
she thought, leaping before she looked?

All too close behind her she heard the scrape of Jethro's
boot on a boulder, heard him say roughly, "Celia—God
almighty, slow down before you break your neck!"

It could have been her father speaking. Don't do this,
don't do that, it's not safe, you'll hurt yourself. She hated
Jethro, hated him. As she swiped at her eyes, her toe hit
an exposed root, tumbling her forward. She flung out her
hands to protect herself and thudded to the ground, her
shoulder crushing the ferns, the dirt scraping her palms.
One cheek struck a rock with bruising force. She cried
out with pain and found she was weeping as though her
heart was broken.

Then Jethro was lifting her. "Are you hurt? Let me see
your face."

There was a note in his voice Celia hadn't heard before;
it had nothing to do with contempt. She burrowed into his
chest, feeling his arms go around her, and sobbed, "He's
dying...don't you *see*? He's dying—that's why I've got
to get m-married."

"Who's dying?"

"My father," she wailed. "Three months, that's what
the doctor says. He and I, we haven't—for once I just
want to be a g-good daughter. Oh Jethro, I don't know
what else to *do*!"

Jethro said incisively, "I don't have a clue what you're
talking about. But this is what we're going to do. I'll carry
you down the rest of the slope, drive you home and clean
up your hands, and then you're going to tell me why you
have to get married because your father's dying.
Here...blow your nose."

A clean white handkerchief was being held to her face.

Celia, who hated being told what to do, blew her nose. "You can't c-carry me, it's too far," she hiccuped.

"Try me."

Kneeling, he gathered her into his arms. Then he stood up and started picking his way down the hill. "And keep quiet," he added. "You've said more than enough in the last ten minutes."

"You sure like giving orders," Celia said, leaning her sore cheek against his chest and closing her eyes.

She felt utterly safe.

She hated safety. So why did it feel like heaven on earth to surrender herself to Jethro? A man—despite what she'd said—she scarcely knew.

Her cheek hurt. So did her hip and her knees and her hands. But it was her pride that was hurt worst of all.

Jethro had said no.

Jethro was breathing hard by the time Celia's Toyota came in sight. He'd let himself get out of shape since K2, he thought, and glanced down at the woman in his arms. Her eyes were shut, tear tracks still streaking her face. Her bare knees were scraped and dirty. There was something so trusting in the way she'd curled herself against his chest; it touched him in a place he very rarely allowed himself to be touched.

With good reason. Women who knew how rich he was weren't to be trusted. In consequence, there was only one kind of touch he allowed from a woman, and it wasn't the emotional kind.

Had he ever been quite so angry as when Celia had asked him—out of the blue—to marry him? What did she think he was—a total fool? And naive as a five-year-old into the bargain? How dare she try and jerk him around like that?

The trouble was, if he was honest, he'd be forced to admit that under his rage was a disappointment bitter enough to choke him. She *was* like the rest. No different from Elisabeth, who'd tried to persuade him she was pregnant and he was the father; or Marliese, who'd threatened him with a lawsuit for breach of promise. Or Candy or Judith or Noreen who'd spent his money like it was going out of style.

Celia—or so he'd thought—was different. She genuinely hadn't seem interested in his money, no matter that she'd read the newspaper article. Nor in pursuing him in any way. Which—again if he were honest—had irritated the hell out of him. He was used to fighting women off. Not chasing after them. But wasn't the decisive way she'd said goodbye last night one of the several reasons he hadn't gotten on the first plane out of here this morning?

But then they'd met on the top of a rocky hill, and she'd seized her chance.

Was it coincidence that they'd met up there? Gun Hill was nothing in the way of a challenge for him; and not much for her, he'd be willing to bet. But of all the places in the area, it was the one where they would most likely meet by chance. Because at some level, he and Celia were alike.

He picked his way over a stream, then skirted a puddle of soggy peat. If she really did have money—and it wouldn't take him long to check that out—then the situation had changed.

Marliese's family had money. Just nowhere near as much money as he had. It hadn't stopped Marliese from trying to sue him.

He'd reached the Toyota. He said, sounding cold and uncaring even to his own ears, "I'm going to put you down, Celia. Where are your keys?"

"In my pocket," she mumbled, pulling back the velcro closing and passing them to him, not meeting his eyes.

They were warm from her body. Scowling, he thrust one into the lock on the passenger side. As he reached for her, she said, "I can manage," and scrambled into the seat.

Don't touch me. That's what she meant. His scowl deepened. He got in the driver's side and put the key in the ignition. "You'll have to give me directions."

"Head back into town. The place I'm renting is on the first street to the right past the fire station. Number forty-two. The door's painted a revolting shade of puce." She then leaned back in the seat and ostentatiously closed her eyes again.

He'd told her to keep quiet. So why was he so angry that she was obeying him? Jethro drove back to Collings Cove, turned right at the fire station and with no difficulty picked out the puce door. "We're here," he said.

Her eyes jerked open. She looked as though she'd just woken from a nightmare to find that the nightmare was still with her, Jethro thought, getting out of the Toyota and following her up the cement path. She was trying very hard not to limp. He found himself staring at her slender waist and the sweet curve of her hips in her shorts as if he hadn't had a woman in six years.

No sex. That was the laugh of the century.

Did she kiss everyone the way she'd kissed him? With such single-minded delight, such generosity?

She couldn't be a virgin. Impossible.

He'd like to kill the guy who'd nearly raped her, and ask questions afterward. If that story was true, and he sensed it was—she surely hadn't been faking the terror with which she'd pushed him away—it would be more than enough to put her off sex. Which meant Pedro really *was* her friend, and her relationship with the doctor *was* platonic.

Jethro rubbed the tension from the back of his neck and walked into her house. The first thing that struck him was the light, streaming through uncurtained windows onto the hardwood floor. What you could see of it. Because the second thing was the mess. Boxes half packed, stuffed garbage bags, piles of clothing and magazines. He said, "Are you usually this untidy?"

"The movers are coming tomorrow, I told you that." She was unlacing her boots. Straightening, she eased them off her feet. "Thank you for driving me home. But I'm okay now, you don't need to stay."

"Considering that less than an hour ago you asked me to marry you, you're in one surefired hurry to get rid of me."

"You said no—remember?"

"I said we'd talk about it after I'd cleaned up your cheek and your knee."

"If the answer's no, there's nothing to talk about!"

She looked ready to explode. He glanced around, then strode over to the alcove by the fireplace and said, gazing at a small painting whose colors glowed like jewels, "That's a Chagall…and over there, it's an early Georgia O'Keeffe, right?"

"They were my mother's. Goodbye, Jethro."

The pottery on the bookshelves was pre-Columbian, he'd bet his shirt. So she did have money. That much was true. And among the books were several he'd read himself and enjoyed. "Where's the first-aid kit?"

"Heaven knows." Her voice rising, Celia added, "I'm perfectly capable of washing a bit of dirt from my face and why can't you take a hint?"

Because I'm not bored.

Jethro stood very still, as if he was the one who'd been hit on the side of the face. Bored? Him? He was never bored, he had a very full life with everything money could buy. A flourishing business empire, acquaintances all round the globe, any woman he wanted when he wanted her. Plus he had his sister and her family whenever he needed a brief stint of domesticity.

Brief was all he could handle. He'd taken over the responsibility for his sister Lindy's welfare when he was nine and she four; their mother was long gone and their father hitting the bottle. For the next sixteen years, until Lindy married, he'd been protector, big brother and surrogate father for Lindy, drastically circumscribing his own life and his freedom to do so.

One more reason he'd never married and had children. Been there, done that.

Celia said irritably, "Now what's the matter?"

Blinking, Jethro came back to the present, to a chestnut-haired woman who looked as if she'd like to pack him into a mover's crate and ship him to Siberia.

A woman who definitely didn't bore him.

Far from it.

CHAPTER FOUR

"I BET the first-aid kit's in the bathroom cupboard," Jethro said, and marched past Celia down the narrow hall.

The shower curtain was splashed with huge red and blue flowers, the floor mat scarlet. He had no idea why a bright red mat should excite him; but it did.

An uncompromising color. A color very sure of itself. Like Celia, he thought, and rummaged in the cupboard. As he located the kit beside a pile of fluffy red towels, Celia stormed up behind him. "Jethro, get out of my house! I apologize, I should never have mentioned the word *marriage*—it was one of the stupidest things I've ever done and I've pulled some dumb stunts in my life. You have every right to be angry with me and will you please leave right now and never come back!"

"I'm not angry," he said calmly, "you're the one who's spitting nickels. And I'm not leaving until you've told me what this is all about. Come on back to the kitchen, the light's better there."

Her shoulders slumped; she suddenly looked exhausted and he remembered with a pang of compunction that she'd worked a twelve-hour shift the night before. In a voice raw with honesty, she said, "Look, I made a mistake. A major one. A really awful one. What are you going to do—make me eat crow? Please don't do that, Jethro."

She wasn't a woman who'd plead for something very often, he knew that in his bones, and fought against the urge to take her in his arms. Don't do it, he thought. Keep your cool. You never had any trouble doing that with Marliese or Elisabeth. So why should it be any different with Celia? He said implacably, ''I want to know more about this proposal of yours.''

''You're like the rock on Gun Hill—immovable,'' she announced, and limped down the hall to the kitchen, plunking herself on a stool so the sun shone full on her scraped cheek. Her lips were set mutinously, her eyes like kindling about to burst into flame.

Jethro washed his hands at the sink. ''You're a bad loser.''

''Tell me how to win when your opponent's made of granite,'' she said, glowering at him as he advanced on her.

''Hold still,'' he said, and very carefully put a wet gauze pad to her cheek. As she winced, his nerves tightened. Her skin was creamy smooth, the hollow under her cheekbone held the soft glow of silk; her lashes were dark, innocent of make-up.

Dirt was ground into the scrape. He worked with exquisite care, watching her clamp her lower lip in her teeth, her face very pale. Finally he said, ''That's got it all, I think. You're going to have one heck of a bruise.''

''I walked into a door, isn't that the usual excuse?'' she snapped, as he smoothed on some antibiotic cream. Then Jethro knelt on the floor, washing her knee. The blue vein down her thigh filled him with such a complexity of emotions that he fumbled the gauze pad, dropping it on the floor. With an impatient exclamation he took another one out of the package.

He lusted after her. That was all. After that big row with Marliese at the ski lodge in Austria last November, he'd steered clear of women. They weren't worth the aggravation.

Sexual deprivation. A very simple explanation for his fierce hunger to possess Celia, to make love to her the night through until she was utterly and completely his. Keep it simple, stupid. It's lust. Nothing to do with her fiery temper and her luscious voice. Or her unique capacity to take him by surprise.

No sex, she'd said. Was that yet one more reason why he'd been so angry with her? How dare she ignore the attraction between them, as if it didn't exist?

"Start talking," he ordered. "What's your father's name and what's wrong with him?"

For a moment Celia hesitated. Jethro looked up; her face was full of uncertainty. He said forcefully, "You cried your eyes out up there on the hill. I don't think you do that often. So it's important to you, this fake marriage."

"You see too much," she whispered. "It scares me when you do that."

He didn't think she scared easy, either. Wanting to kiss her so badly he could almost taste the sweetness of her lips, he said harshly, "Get on with it."

Her lips compressed. "My father's name is Ellis Scott. Ellis Scott III. Old Washington money. He's got a rare form of leukemia."

"Marrying me—or anyone else for that matter—won't cure leukemia," Jethro said more gently, removing the last flake of mica from her grazed knee.

"I know that." She sighed. "After my mother died, he became so over-protective I could scarcely breathe. Yet at the same time, he was emotionally distant. Cold. Controlling. It was awful. I could have made the state junior slalom team when I was fourteen, but he wouldn't put up the money. Too risky. Play tennis instead. So as an adolescent I majored in rebellion, and when I was nineteen we had a huge bust-up. Then there was no contact between us for several years. A while ago, after I had my own money and this job, I got in touch with him again, and we've seen each other several times since then. It's not what you'd call a great relationship, but it's sure better than nothing. Much better."

Jethro hadn't had any kind of relationship with his father; his mother, for as long as she'd hung around, had been more interested in her lovers than in her two children. "Now he wants you to get married," he said in a neutral voice, taking the cap off the antibiotic again.

"So I'll be safe and secure. Like my brother, who's conservative and contented and always does everything right." She gave another heavy sigh. "But I'm older now, and my father's dying, and surely it wouldn't hurt me to get married for three months. To relieve his mind. I'm not saying he's right to want me married—he isn't. I'm my own security, although I don't suppose he'd understand that in a million years." She gave Jethro a troubled look. "Do you understand?"

It was a strange time to feel as though he were poised over an abyss. Trust her, one voice whispered. Look at her, she's honest as the day's long. Not a mercenary bone in her body. Check her out, another voice insisted. You know your net worth. You can't trust anyone around that kind of money. Sure, she's got skin you're aching to stroke and an infinitely kissable mouth and brown eyes that seem to go straight to your soul. But what do you really know about her?

Maybe she wants to be on her father's good side to make sure she inherits when he dies.

He'd hesitated too long. She said, her lashes dropping to hide her eyes, "I guess you don't."

He said brusquely, "So this would be a marriage for appearances only."

"No sex. No prying into each other's lives. And when he dies, it's over. An uncontested divorce and no more contact."

His surge of rage was utterly irrational. Jethro stood up, then pulled her to her feet, standing very close to her. He rested his palms on her shoulders, kneading her skin with a rhythmic insistence, letting his gaze wander from the curve of her lips to the thrust of her breasts under her T-shirt. But he didn't kiss her. Not yet. "No sex. You're sure about that?"

"Yes," she said, overly loudly.

"Maybe it's time you tried going to bed with someone other than the creep who nearly raped you."

"Sex isn't something you try—like a pair of shoes you're thinking of buying! I'm going to be in love with the next man I go to bed with. Not that that's any of your business."

She wasn't in love with the doctor; he'd only had to see them together to know that. Jethro said briskly, "I need to think about it until tomorrow. I'll get back to you in the morning. Will you be here?"

"But on Gun Hill you said no."

"I might change my mind."

Suddenly she looked frightened. "If you can change your mind, I can change mine."

"It's too late for that," he said in a hard voice. "You wouldn't be asking me—a perfect stranger—if you had a dozen other candidates all lined up. If I say yes, then we'll get married. Is that clear?"

She took a step back. "I...I don't—"

"If you didn't want to marry me, you shouldn't have asked."

She didn't just look frightened, she looked terrified out of her wits. And for once she had nothing to say. Good, Jethro thought meanly. "I'll drop by tomorrow morning with my answer. Either way. Yes or no." Giving her a curt nod, he headed for the door.

She followed him. "But—but your vehicle, it's back at the north—"

"I need the exercise. And jogging always helps me think." Before she could say anything else, he turned, took her chin in his hands and kissed her, thoroughly, with all the technical skill at his command.

While he still had control—just—he pulled back. How's that for a new challenge, Jethro, not to fall all over her, this woman with chestnut hair that smells of flowers? "See you tomorrow morning," he said. "Good luck with the cupboards."

Then he let himself out. But he didn't head in the direction of Gun Hill. He went back to his motel, where he jotted down a few notes, then picked up the phone.

The movers arrived sharp at nine in the morning. Celia felt like the bottom of a bird cage and looked worse. Her muscles had stiffened overnight; her shoulder, her knee and her cheek were interesting blends of purple, pink and mustard yellow, and she'd scarcely slept a wink.

But at 5:00 a.m. she'd come to one conclusion. If Jethro said yes—which he almost certainly wouldn't—then she'd go ahead with this fake marriage.

She'd phoned her father yesterday evening, in between boxing all her food for her next-door neighbor and tackling the hall cupboard. Although Ellis's voice sounded a little weaker, he'd been—she'd swear—glad to hear from her. She didn't have much time to repair the damage of years, and if a marriage would help that process, then married she'd be. It would be worth it.

The movers, whose names were Joe and Jim, had eyed her cheek curiously and gotten to work. It was going to be a very hot day, atypically warm for September.

Even though Celia was busy all morning, the time passed with agonizing slowness. Suspense was far from the most comfortable of emotions, she thought, wishing Jethro would arrive, wondering why he hadn't.

By 11:45, she'd decided he'd skipped town: he'd caught the early flight because he couldn't wait to see the last of her. She scarcely knew whether to be relieved or disappointed that he'd reneged. He was dangerous, she knew that; she'd known it from the first moment she'd seen him on her television monitor at work. He was also pure male, every inch of him, with a good dash of the predator thrown in. To say he was sexy was like saying a teddy bear was cuddly.

And she really did know very little about him, he was right about that. Instead of scrubbing her dirty oven, she'd have been better off phoning her lawyer in Washington to check on him.

Easy, she thought with a throb of relief, I'll do it right now. Just because I banged my knee doesn't mean my brain has to go on hold. And a break would do me good, I can't believe how hot it is today.

The doorbell rang, a loud peal that scraped all Celia's nerves. The Salvation Army, she thought frantically, come to pick up my old clothes, and opened the door. "Hello, Jethro," she said faintly. "I thought you weren't coming."

He was wearing a blue cotton shirt with the sleeves rolled back, and faded jeans; his hair shone with cleanliness. "It took longer than I thought to get some of the answers I was looking for. Let's go for lunch, Celia. Sally owes you a piece of pie."

"Lunch? I can't—I'm a mess."

Her shorts were fuchsia, her shirt a wild swirl of fuchsia, green and yellow, and her hair was tumbling in untidy curls around her face. The bruise on her cheek was also yellow. "You look fine to me," Jethro said.

There was something in his voice that made her flush from more than the heat. Then Joe called out, "You go for lunch, missis, we're about ready to eat, too."

"Good," said Jethro, and seven minutes later Sally was ushering them to one of the window seats. The air-conditioning, for once, was working. Sally was inclined to linger, giving Jethro her best smile as she passed him the menu and poured two glasses of water. Celia said, "I'll have a club sandwich on whole wheat, please, and a Coke with lots of ice."

"Hamburger with the works and a beer," Jethro said. "Thanks, Sally." Then he leaned back in his chair and gave Celia a lazy grin. "I'm old-fashioned. I'd want you to go by Celia Lathem."

With exaggerated care she put down her glass of water. Her voice seemed to come from a long way away. "You mean you'll do it?"

"For better or for worse."

She stared at him as though she'd never seen him before. He's a man, she thought weakly. Just a man. So his hair gleams in the sun, and his face is as strongly carved as granite, and his mouth...don't think about what his mouth does to you, Celia, not a smart move. She said edgily, "You agree to all my conditions?"

He reached in the pocket of his jacket and drew out a couple of pieces of paper. "I had my lawyer fax me a contract."

"Jethro, it's up to me to draw up the contract!"

"Just wanted to show you I was serious," he said blandly.

"I'm the one who's doing the hiring—not the other way round," she said, and grabbed the papers from him. The typescript ran together, making very little sense. *No sex* seemed to have been translated into something called an *abrogation of conjugal relations*; her insistence on privacy had become a long-winded phrase about *no unnecessary intrusions into the affairs, business, personal or otherwise of the other party as heretofore defined in section three*.

Jethro said agreeably, "We could both sign it—that way I'll know you're serious, too. Once we're in Washington, you could get your lawyer to check it out."

She said tightly, "Speaking of which—I presume you checked me out."

"Absolutely."

A large Coke was put in front of Celia, who looked at it as if she weren't quite sure what it was. She gave Sally a distracted smile. "Thanks."

"You're welcome. Boss says it's on the house along with the chocolate cream pie."

"That's sweet of him, Sally...thanks." As Sally rather reluctantly departed for another table, Celia added, "And what did you find out?"

Jethro raised his glass. "To wedded bliss, my darling Celia." His eyes were full of mockery.

"I'm not your darling!"

"You'll have to pretend you are in front of your father. It wouldn't hurt to practise a bit."

Her jaw dropped. She'd never thought that far ahead; she'd been too caught up in worrying about who would marry her to think about how she'd behave once she found someone. She said in a furious undertone, "Let's get something straight, Jethro. I'm in control here. I'm hiring you, for pay, to do a job. I'm the employer, you're the employee.... Have you got that?"

"A cool sixty thousand," he said. "Amazing what money'll do."

She tossed her curls. "You presumably found out that the money's real—that I'm not stringing you a line."

"Ellis Bartlett Scott III. He inherited wealth and he's been shrewd enough to multiply it several times over. Reputation as a fair man, dead honest, not much sense of humor. His son takes after him. His daughter...ah, now we come to the interesting part."

Jethro took a gulp of his beer. "Wild. Expelled from so many schools I lost count. All the very best schools, mind you. Expert skier, degree in languages from Harvard, travelled round the world on a shoestring working as a waitress. Ended up in Canada. Graduated from the Coast Guard college. Inherited her mother's trust fund, got her pilot's licence and bought her own plane. Yeah, you could say I checked up on you."

A clubhouse sandwich was put in front of Celia. Her appetite had totally deserted her. Jethro added, "With all that going on, she hasn't had much time for men. There was mention of a guy called Darryl Coates. Is he the one who tried to rape you?"

She hesitated a fraction too long. "So he is," Jethro finished in a hard voice.

Celia shivered; she wouldn't put it past Jethro to take his own revenge on Darryl. "I didn't say so."

"You don't have to. Darryl's recently divorced rich wife number one and he's on the lookout—"

"He *is*?"

"Oh, didn't you know that, Celia? Would you have

married him rather than me in spite of what he did to you? Too late now, I've accepted your offer."

She felt like a mouse being toyed with by a cat. Determined not to show that the claws had drawn blood, she said, "Then perhaps it's fortunate I didn't know. Since you can use the cash."

As she put salt on her fries and started to eat, Jethro said, "The only other man in your life is your doctor friend. Who'd jump at the chance to marry you."

"He's not going to have the chance. I told you—he's in love with me."

"All the more reason to marry him, I'd have thought."

"I'm sure you would."

"And what's that supposed to mean?" Jethro demanded.

"I marry Paul who's in love with me and then in three months say goodbye, Paul, it's been nice knowing you, have a happy divorce? I don't think so."

"But that's what you'll be saying to me."

"You're different." Her gaze was level. "I may not know a whole lot about you, but I'm sure you can look after yourself."

His breath hissed between his teeth; she'd gotten to him, Celia realized with a primitive thrill of triumph. Going on the offensive, she said crisply, "Your lawyer hasn't covered the times of payment. Half when we get to Washington, right after the wedding. The other half after you move out. Certified cheques."

"And what if your father takes an instant dislike to me?"

"You'll have to make sure he doesn't, won't you?" she said with a brilliant smile.

Jethro said unpleasantly, "Of course, I've got class, haven't I? Isn't that what you said when you were listing my assets as a potential husband?'' He glanced down at the paper place mat and cheap cutlery. ''I know enough to use my fork for the fries and not to lick my fingers.''

''That's not what I meant! You make me sound like a horrible snob.''

''So what did you mean, Celia?''

''It's the way you hold yourself, your...confidence,'' she stumbled, ''your air of command. As though you're a lot more than the skipper of a sloop.''

His lashes flickered. She'd touched another nerve, she thought, puzzled. With more assurance, she went on, ''I'll add a codicil to your contract that it's only a temporary document, and I'll get a new one drawn up in Washington before the wedding. This is a great sandwich...how's the burger?''

''How did we meet?'' Jethro asked.

She blinked. ''We'll tell the truth—I'm a lousy liar, I'll only trip myself up if we invent something. You came here to thank me after *Starspray* sank. Simple.''

''And we fell in love,'' said Jethro in an unreadable voice.

''That's right,'' she said, brown eyes clashing with steel-blue. ''Love at first sight. We knew we were meant for each other, and we fell into each other's arms. Soulmates from the start. Terribly romantic.''

''Bedmates from the start, too.''

''That,'' she said insouciantly, ''is where the acting comes in.'' She grinned at him. ''When I was at Harvard, I used to read romance novels at exam time to take the pressure off...you'd make a very good hero. And if I ever get to a decent hairdresser, I might not look so bad as the heroine.''

''Except that in our case the hero and heroine will live

happily ever after for no more than three months…it's all a game to you, isn't it?''

She flinched at the savagery in his tone. "A game with a very serious purpose," she said. "I'd rather you not forget that. And after all, you did buy into it, Jethro.''

"Why not? What have I got to lose?''

She hated his mockery. Scrabbling in her purse for a pen, Celia picked up his contract and added the codicil. Then she read the whole document thoroughly before she signed it. "Your turn," she said, passing it to Jethro.

His signature was illegible, a very masculine scrawl. "Well," she said inadequately, "step one.''

"I wonder what step thirteen will be," Jethro said softly.

She didn't want to think as far ahead as step two, let alone thirteen. With great determination, she started telling him about some of her more hair-raising shifts with the Coast Guard, after which he described his passage through the Straits of Magellan; and the whole time their words were nothing but camouflage over a seethe of emotions Celia couldn't begin to describe or subdue. Then they ate their pie, and Sally bid Celia a tearful goodbye.

As they drove back to the town house, Celia said, "I've got the staff farewell dinner tonight. I'll be ready to leave by ten tomorrow morning, the forecast's good, and I'm sure if we're soulmates you'll trust me to fly you safely to Washington. So I'll see you at the motel around nine-thirty.''

"Fine," said Jethro, and pulled up outside the puce door.

But before she could get out, he took her by the shoulders and pulled her toward him. She gasped, "What are you—"

"We need the practice," he said, and kissed her with an incendiary mixture of anger and passion.

Every nerve she possessed sprang to life. If she was no good at lying, she was no good at deception either, thought Celia, and kissed him back, opening to him, her tongue dancing with his, the heat of his hands burning through her shirt. Her breasts were hard against his chest, her fingers—somehow—had tangled themselves in his hair, and her whole body felt pliant, like beach grass in a wind from the sea.

Behind them came three blasts of a horn. Jim and Joe, she thought confusedly, in the moving van. She shoved at Jethro's chest and unwisely said the first thing that came into her head. "We don't need practice. We do just fine without it."

The pulse at the neck of his shirt was pounding, as though he'd carried her all the way up Gun Hill. She watched it, fascinated, wondering if his skin would taste of salt, her nostrils filled with the scent of his body: soap, aftershave, and something else that was unique to Jethro and that she'd recognize anywhere.

What was happening to her?

She scrambled out of the Nissan, trying to look calm and collected, and slammed the door with unnecessary force.

There was one piece of information she hadn't given Jethro. Tonight she'd be staying at the same motel as he. She'd booked a room for after the staff dinner.

She should have asked for the room farthest from his.

No sex. No conjugal relations.

She'd put her signature on a contract to that effect. She'd do well to remember it.

CHAPTER FIVE

IF SHE hadn't signed a contract that afternoon agreeing to marry a man who fascinated, attracted and terrified her, Celia would have enjoyed herself at the staff dinner. She was wearing her prettiest dress and had openly made a joke of her bruised and scraped cheek. Her boss's speech was complimentary, and her coworkers were in the mood to party.

Paul was also there. Paul was making no attempt to look as though he were enjoying himself. She'd made the mistake, a month or so ago, of issuing him a rather generalized invitation to Washington; to her consternation, he'd announced ten minutes ago that he was planning to come for a weekend in October. So she was going to have to tell him about Jethro.

She didn't have a clue how she was going to do that.

She and Paul had dated quite a while before he'd as much as kissed her. Pleasant kisses, that aroused none of the terror of Darryl's or the passion of Jethro's. Jethro's kisses were temporary insanity, a madness of the body. Like eating jalapeño peppers or vindaloo curry.

She wasn't going to think about Jethro. She'd have lots of time for that tomorrow.

Despite the lack of sparks between her and Paul, she liked him very much; for a while, she had thought she could change this liking into something deeper and more lasting, that an affair between her and Paul would catapult her into that blissful state called *being in love*, a state her friends seemed to achieve with astonishing ease.

Unfortunately, Paul's kisses had never caused her to lose her head, not in the slightest degree. Consequently, she'd stayed out of his bed.

She was very fond of Paul. *Fond*, Celia thought, what a wishy-washy word.

It was one o'clock in the morning and she was tired. But Paul was obviously going to outwait everyone else at the party to make sure he said goodbye to her in private. Get it over with, Celia, she decided, and started a round of goodbyes. Then she said to Paul, "Are you leaving now?"

He stood up. He wasn't as tall as Jethro, his face open where Jethro's was guarded, his eyes now as miserable as a neglected dog's. Stifling a sigh, Celia led the way outside. "I can't believe how warm it still is," she said, "I thought I'd melt while I was packing all those boxes."

"You had lunch today with that guy," Paul said in a hostile voice. "The one whose boat sank."

She should have known there'd be no secrets in Collings Cove. But he'd given her the perfect opening. "Yes, I did. I had some...business to discuss with him."

"Business? What kind of business?"

It wasn't like Paul to be so truculent. "Remember I told you my father was ill? But I didn't tell you he made what I suppose could be called a last request. He wants me to get married before he dies, he thinks that'll settle me down and—"

"I'll marry you," said Paul.

"No, Paul—we've been through all that before. Anyway, I don't want to settle down, I'm not ready to." She swallowed. "So I'm going to enter into a fake marriage. Just until my father dies. With Jethro. Paul, I'm sorry, but I have to do this for my father's sake, please try to understand."

Paul was staring at her as if she'd just said she was pregnant with quintuplets. "You're going to marry a man you hadn't even *met* three days ago?"

Put like that, it didn't sound very sensible. In fact, it sounded totally off the wall. "Jethro's not in love with me, he's got an ego as tough as sealskin, and he's an adventurer like me. Besides, we've signed a legal contract. It's a business deal, Paul. Nothing more."

"I can see why you'd prefer him to me," Paul said bitterly.

Jethro's charisma, she thought. So Paul had noticed. "That's got nothing to do with it."

"You're out of your mind."

"I'm not—I'm just doing the best I can to make my father's last months happy ones."

"You're making a bad mistake! I've seen the guy. He's not some half-baked bureaucrat from St. John's, he's a big-time operator—he'll take you to the cleaners."

Her heart sank. Because she was afraid Paul was right? "No, he won't. My lawyers will see to that."

"Did he hit you? Is that why your cheek's a mess?"

"Of course not! I told you, I tripped when I was on Gun Hill."

"Have you been to bed with him?"

"No. No sex, it's in the contract."

"No sex? That guy? You think he'll take no for an answer? Sorry, dear, I have a headache...that'll really impress him. Get real, Celia."

"Oh, do shut up!"

"You can't move people around like they're stones on the beach," Paul said, "it doesn't work. Tear up the contract, tell your dad you're not ready to get married but that you've quit your job to be with him until he dies, and go from there. I bet that'll set his mind to rest."

"You don't know my father," she said caustically.

"I'm beginning to think I don't know you," Paul retorted. "Don't do it, Celia. Call it off while you still can. Jethro Lathem's no tame puppy dog who'll heel when you tell him to. He's a wolf of the first order. With teeth."

It wasn't the time to remember how her tongue had flicked against Jethro's teeth, how her body had melted into his as if she were a candle on fire. "I can look after myself," she said, inwardly wondering how true that was. "Paul, I had to tell you sooner or later, and I wanted to do it face-to-face."

"You're not going to change your mind, are you?"

Jethro wouldn't let her. With a strange sense of fatality, she said, "It's too late for that."

"Then I wish you luck."

His sarcasm was forgivable. There was no point in prolonging this, Celia thought. She shouldn't have told Paul. She should have lied by omission and withdrawn her invitation for his visit to Washington, stressing that it was better they go their separate ways. She said quietly, "Goodbye, Paul. I'm sorry I couldn't fall in love with you, truly I am. If you ever feel like writing to me, I'd like to hear from you. And please…be happy."

Paul made no move to kiss her. "Goodbye," he said stiffly, and turned toward his Jeep.

Celia was driving Wayne's second car, an old jalopy that rattled like a can of bolts; the man to whom she'd sold her Toyota had picked it up that afternoon. She drove away, doing her best to forget the injured look on Paul's face.

Everything would have been so easy if only she'd fallen in love with him. But although she felt regret now parting from Paul, it was only regret—nothing stronger. What was wrong with her? In some real way, she thought moodily, she was a failure as a woman. Something was missing in her, something crucial: the ability to fall in love. Was it because her mother had died when she was only five and her father had retreated from her that she was now incapable of the deep love a marriage required? Why couldn't she fall in love and commit herself to a partnership that would expand her horizons, give her passion, happiness and children?

She'd like to have children. Some day.

But marriage had always felt too constricting. And why fall in love if the end result was the kind of grief her father had suffered for as long as she could remember? Her mother's death had destroyed Ellis Scott. Was love worth that risk?

Into her tired mind dropped the image she'd remembered since she was perhaps four and a half. It was spring. She'd been playing under the cherry trees in the back garden of Fernleigh and had run toward the house to show her mother the pink petals she'd found in the grass. But then she'd stopped near the boxwood hedge. Her mother and father were standing on the steps below the conservatory, a red silk shawl draped around her mother's shoulders. She was leaning back against her husband, whose arms were locked around her waist; the last rays of the sun caught in her chestnut hair. She had looked utterly beautiful, like a fairy princess in the embrace of her prince.

Was that image one more reason Celia had kept herself separate from the casual affairs of her classmates at Harvard and the Coast Guard college? Did she crave the depth and intensity of love that she'd glimpsed as a child that long-ago evening under the pale mist of the cherry trees?

At one time she'd thought she might fall in love with

Darryl. Since then, she'd tried her best to do the same with Paul. But, she thought, cheering up, there was no chance in the world she'd fall in love with Jethro. Despite what Paul had said, she wasn't that crazy.

The window of Wayne's car was stuck shut and the heater, no matter where she shoved the lever, was belting out malodorous hot air. But at least Jethro wouldn't connect her with this old rattletrap.

By the time she reached the motel, Celia's cheeks were pink and her hair sticking to her forehead. It was one-thirty and the motel was quiet. Jethro's Nissan was parked at the far end, she noticed with considerable relief.

Her room was stuffy. As she pushed back the curtains, she caught sight of the pool out back; it was gleaming like a mirror under the outside lights. Empty.

A swim. That's what she needed. To wash off Paul's warnings and her own fears; to rid herself of a day that seemed to have gone on forever.

She rummaged in her duffel bag and five minutes later was letting herself out the back door, the key pinned to the strap of her tight-fitting white maillot. She dove neatly into the deep end and started doing lengths in a smooth overarm crawl, back and forth, until the tension eased from her shoulders, and both guilt and fear had dissolved in the chlorine-laced water. Only then did she roll over on her back.

Only then did she see the man standing on the edge of the pool, watching her.

As she gave an involuntary gasp of alarm, she realized it was Jethro. He was wearing dark trunks. His body was magnificent—his belly corded with muscle, his legs long and tightly muscled. The curl of dark hair on his chest, the width of his shoulders, the taut column of his throat, filled her with a confusion of panic and desire; her hard-earned peace evaporated like water in the heat of the sun.

Jethro had been watching Celia swim for several minutes; he'd suspected she'd be staying here tonight once the movers had taken her furniture, and he'd been keeping an eye out for her. She swam as gracefully as a porpoise, the sleek curves of her body moving economically through the dark water; when she rolled over, he saw the tight buds of her nipples through the wet fabric of her suit. Saw, too, her start of alarm. "Hello, Celia," he said. "How was the party?"

After a fractional hesitation, she said breathlessly, "Great. I'll race you—ten lengths."

He dove in, surfacing only inches away from her. Her hair was slicked to her skull, her dark eyes laughing at him; it had taken her only a couple of seconds to recover from the fright of suddenly seeing him. No kittenish shrieks of alarm, no pouting, no batting of her wet lashes. Just laughter. Laughter and a dare.

I like the way you operate, he thought.

He had no intention of telling her so. "You're on," Jethro said. "Ready, set, go."

He was a good swimmer, both taller and stronger than Celia; he finished first by half a length. Gripping the edge of the pool with one hand, he said, "We forgot to discuss the prize."

"You're slipping," she said amiably. "You'll have to make do with the satisfaction of knowing you won. Won a race in the pool, that is."

"In a few days I'm going to win the hand of the rich and beautiful heroine."

"But only her hand. Not the rest of her."

"Oh Celia," Jethro drawled, "you do believe in dares, don't you?"

"It beats settling down with a husband and one point eight kids," she said, took a deep breath and sank below the water.

Jethro hauled himself out of the pool, sitting beside the ladder as he watched for her to reappear. Contract or no contract, he was going to make love to Celia Scott. He was going to kiss her until she whimpered with need in his arms, caress her until she begged him for completion; and she'd enjoy it every bit as much as he.

He was quite prepared to wait. He didn't yet know when it would happen. Certainly not before the wedding, in case she called the whole thing off. But happen it would, and in a time and place of his choosing.

She'd be worth waiting for. He'd swear to that.

He'd never waited for a woman before. Never had to. What he'd wanted he'd taken, and the woman had always been willing. So why, this time, was he content to bide his time?

She'd been under the water a long time, he thought suddenly.

Even as he felt the first prickle of anxiety, she surfaced at the far end of the pool. She smiled at him, her teeth gleaming white. Then she sank again, and a few moments later he could see her swimming toward him underwater, her limbs exquisitely proportioned, all her movements imbued with an entirely feminine strength and grace. Her long hair streamed out behind her.

He wanted her hair spread on his pillow, her face flushed with desire. He wanted to kiss her breasts, her belly, the sweet hollow of her spine until his body was scented with hers, her beauty unforgettably imprinted in his flesh.

Unforgettably? He always forgot his women.

She burst out of the water at his feet in a flurry of spray. "Only ten lengths, Jethro, and you're taking a rest?" she gasped. "Are you a man or a mouse?"

Kneeling, he reached down and lifted her out of the pool in one swift motion, his biceps hard as the concrete around the pool. Then he straightened, drawing her to stand beside him. "I'll let you be the judge of that," he said, and kissed her.

She tasted of chlorine, her wet swimsuit cold against his chest. Her breasts were firm, the jut of her hipbones exciting him as though she was his very first woman and all this was new to him. His kiss deepened, his tongue seeking hers, his hands pulling her closer until she could be in no doubt that he wanted her.

She quivered like a high-strung racehorse at the starting gate, kissing him back with the recklessness that was so much a part of her. A recklessness that until now, if he trusted her word, she'd never allowed herself to feel with a man.

Could it be true? Could he believe her?

He wanted to, desperately. Wanted her to be his and his alone.

He groaned her name, sliding his lips down her throat, one hand cupping the curve of her breast. His head was doing the swimming, he thought crazily, and thrust with his body, hardness to softness, male to female.

Much more of this and he'd be totally out of control. Which wasn't part of his strategy. Not yet. He fought for breath, easing away from her, and somehow found his voice. "What's the verdict, Celia? Man or mouse?"

She was panting; in a primitive thrill of pride, he knew the beat of her pulse was nothing to do with her laps in the pool and everything to do with him. And this time she hadn't pulled away. She said shakily, "Skip the mouse. How about a tidal wave?"

"We didn't cover those in the contract."

"I'll alert my lawyer."

He put his hands on her shoulders; her bones were, paradoxically, both delicate and strong. "What time did you say we're leaving in the morning?"

"Nine-thirty."

"We can drive in the Nissan. It's a rental. I'll drop it off at the airport." As she nodded wordlessly, he added, "We'd better go to bed. Full day tomorrow."

Suddenly she shivered. "Jethro, I won't—"

"Separate beds," he said in a cutting voice. "And remember something, will you? I'm not Darryl. I'll never make you do anything you don't want to do."

"I'm cold," she muttered, "I've got to have a shower. Good night, Jethro."

"Good night, Celia," he said, and watched the seductive swing of her hips as she headed for the door of her unit.

It would give him infinite pleasure to undo the damage that bastard Darryl Coates had caused her. To strip from her any vestige of fear and reluctance, setting free the woman of passion that she really was. To strip her naked, body and soul.

And she'd be willing. Oh yes, this time she'd be willing.

The following afternoon, Celia hauled the last piece of luggage out of her Cessna, which was parked on the tarmac of a private airstrip outside Washington. It had been an ideal day for a long-distance flight, with tail winds the whole way and perfect visibility. Patting the fuselage affectionately, she gave Jethro an uncomplicated smile of pure pleasure. "I love this plane. Sort of like you and *Starspray*, I suppose."

"You're a good pilot," he said sincerely. "I enjoyed that."

She flushed with pleasure; Jethro wasn't a man to hand out superfluous compliments. "Thanks...we'll have to go through customs. Then my father's chauffeur should be here to meet us."

"And the game begins," Jethro said lightly.

She frowned. "You sure know how to bring me back down to earth with a thud."

He laughed and put an arm round her shoulders. "Smile, Celia. From now on, my darling, we're lovers. Crazy about each other, in bed and out."

"Lay off—no one can see us out here!"

He raised one brow. "We're supposed to be in love. You can't go turning it off whenever it suits you—glaring at me as though you hate my guts one minute, and madly in love with me the next. We'll be caught out in no time if you do that. You've fallen for me, Celia. You're bringing me home to meet your father and you're deliriously happy."

"Deliriously happy," she repeated in an inimical voice.

"You got it."

Her face felt as stiff as cardboard, and a chunk of ice had lodged itself in the vicinity of her stomach. It was all very well to be reckless. But—and she should have remembered this, she'd been expelled from enough schools for the lesson to have sunk in—recklessness usually brought in its aftermath certain consequences.

She'd proposed to Jethro. He'd accepted. And now she had to act as though she were in love with him.

"Three months," she said. "It sounds like a life sentence."

"You're doing it for your father...remember?" Jethro lashed.

...who was under a sentence of death. Celia flushed with shame. How could she have forgotten? What was it about Jethro that drove everything else out of her mind but him? "Of course I remember," she snapped. "Let's go. The sooner we get this charade under way, the better. The chauffeur's name's Mason. He's been with my father since before I was born, and he has three grandchildren he adores."

"So let's go and play the game, sweetheart."

She whirled to face him. "Don't call me that!"

He gripped her elbow, his fingers digging into her flesh. "Why not?"

She said in a rush, "Darryl called me baby. Paul called me dear. You can call me baby and dear and darling twenty-four hours a day if that's what turns you on. But not sweetheart."

"Who called you sweetheart?" Jethro asked, dropping each word like a stone.

No one had. That was the trouble. It was an endearment she privately adored, and if ever she fell in love, she wanted it kept for a happiness and a man she couldn't even begin to imagine. "Never you mind," she retorted childishly.

"There's been another man, hasn't there? One you're not telling me about."

She shrank from the fury in his face. But not for anything was she going to reveal to him daydreams as fragile as cherry petals. "How many women have you had, Jethro?" she flared. "Are you going to tell me about each and every one of them?"

"You'll tell me about him," Jethro threatened. "Sooner or later."

"There's nothing to tell," she cried, and wondered why the truth should sound so unconvincing. "Let's go—Mason will be wondering where we are."

"We're making mad, passionate love behind the hangar," Jethro said savagely. "Right, Celia?"

She was determined not to show how much he frightened her. She must have been mad to propose to him; Paul was right, Jethro was a predator and teeth were the very least of his weapons. She said with only the slightest quiver in her voice, "Be careful, Jethro Lathem. You haven't got your first paycheck, and I can still change my mind."

"I'll sue you if you try."

"You wouldn't!"

His short laugh held nothing of amusement. "Oh yes, I would. Breach of promise."

Celia stood very still, the heat of the sun beating up from the tarmac, her body ice-cold. "You mean it, don't you?"

"A lawsuit wouldn't be a very edifying experience for your father. You might want to think about that."

He did mean it. Every word. "What have I done?" Celia whispered. "What in heaven's name have I done?"

"You've agreed to marry me for as long as your father lives," Jethro said with brutal emphasis. "Let's get on with it."

The pavement shimmered and there wasn't a breath of breeze; for a moment Celia wondered if she was going to faint. She'd been reckless once too often, she thought numbly. Jethro Lathem was the last man on earth she should have chosen.

And it was too late. That's what he was saying. Too late to change her mind.

CHAPTER SIX

WITH AN incoherent exclamation, Celia headed for the customs shed; ten minutes later she and Jethro emerged into the sunshine again. Mason was standing beside the Mercedes.

Act, Celia. Act.

She took Jethro by the arm, and pulled him forward. "Mason," she said, giving the chauffeur a quick hug, "lovely to see you. I have a surprise, a wonderful surprise—this is my brand-new fiancé, Jethro Lathem."

"Well, Miss Celia, congratulations," Mason said. "Never thought I'd see the day. You've got yourself a fine woman, Mr. Lathem. The very best...congratulations to you too, sir."

Jethro drew Celia into the circle of his arm. "Thanks, Mason. I'm a very lucky guy."

It was done, thought Celia. She had announced herself as Jethro's fiancée and she couldn't back out now. The word would be all through the house as soon as they got home, and then there'd be the crucial interview with her father.

She was going to marry a perfect stranger who wasn't perfect at all. Just the opposite, in fact. Then Jethro nudged her, saying, "Right, darling?"

"Sorry," she stumbled, "I was daydreaming...so much has happened the last few days, Mason, I'm still breathless." Fluttering her lashes at Jethro, she did her best to look like a woman whom love had rendered starry-eyed and absent-minded.

Jethro dropped a quick kiss on her lips. "Let's go home, Celia—I want to meet your father. I'm sure we'll have a lot in common."

She wished she were as sure. And how dare he say *home*? It wasn't his home, it was hers. She said pleasantly, "This is all the luggage we have, Mason, the movers are delivering the rest of my stuff next week. How is my father?"

"Looking forward to seeing you, miss," Mason replied and opened the car door for her.

Jethro climbed in beside her and put his arm round her shoulders, pulling her close. As Mason took his seat, she smiled sleepily at her so-called beloved. "I'm going to have a snooze, honey, I'm wiped," she said and, with wicked delight, saw him cringe. She'd been pretty sure he'd hate being called honey. Hurray, she thought vengefully and closed her eyes.

Nor did she open them until Mason turned into the tall gates of Fernleigh. The house, as always, both welcomed Celia with long familiarity and repelled her with its formality. Yet its stone facade, Corinthian columns, and symmetry of blank windows, together with a garden whose rigidity put Versailles to shame, were home to her, the only real home she'd ever had. Jethro murmured into her ear, "We're a long way from the Seaview Grill."

His breath was warm, wafting across her skin; involuntary pleasure rippled along her nerves. She said with a brightness that sounded as fake as her proposed marriage, "I'm so anxious for you to meet my father, Jethro. We'll go straight up."

The wide staircase was flanked with portraits of ancestors who didn't look any happier to be there than she was. "When I was six," she prattled, "I got up on the ladder the window cleaners were using and painted a moustache on my great-great-grandfather—the one in the black coat who looks like he's attending a wake. I got spanked for that.''

"I'm scarcely in the door and I can see this is no house for a child," Jethro said harshly. "Was that after your mother died?"

"Seven months later."

"I'm beginning to understand all those expulsions…what the hell was your father thinking of?"

"Why are you so angry?" Celia asked, puzzled. "He loved my mother. He never got over her death."

"So you're determined not to fall in love in case the same thing happens to you. Tell me I'm wrong."

She tossed her head. "My father's portrait is the one at the top of the stairs."

Jethro took her by the shoulders, his voice gravelly with suppressed emotion. "I suggest you have your lawyer amend the privacy clause. Because I'm going to get a few answers out of you while I'm here."

"The way I was brought up isn't your concern and we aren't going to have a fight two minutes before you meet my father!"

"Then let's see what we can do to shock your great-great-grandfather," Jethro said, and kissed her parted lips with a fierce intimacy that scorched her cheeks with color and made her heart hammer in her breast. Then he let her go so suddenly she staggered. "That feels a whole lot better," he said. "Let's beard the lion in his den. Which way?"

Celia blurted, "You're just like me." A rebel. Uncaring of convention or propriety.

"Are you only just figuring that out?" Jethro's smile didn't quite reach his eyes. "That's why you're so madly in love with me."

"I should have met you when I was six. Not now," she announced, and stalked along the marble-tiled hall. Her father's suite of rooms was at the back of the house, with a view of the topiary and the knot gardens, everything pruned and rigidly under control. Outside his door, she suddenly stopped. "I—I haven't told him about you yet. I'd better go in first and break the news."

"Oh no, my darling. We're in this together." With a wolfish smile, Jethro gestured for her to precede him.

Chewing on her lip, Celia tapped on the door. "Come in," her father called.

With the sense she was embarking on a long flight without navigation equipment or altimeter, Celia walked into Ellis Scott's private living room. Her father was sitting by the window. Using the arm of the chair for support, he stood up to greet her. His iron-gray hair had a military cut, the creases in his trousers were knife-sharp, and his tie bore the emblem of an ivy-league university. "Hello, Father," Celia said, crossed the room and kissed him on the cheek.

"So you've finally come home," he said. "Good. I can keep an eye on you here. What happened to your face?"

She'd done her best to hide the marks on her cheek with makeup. "I fell when I was hiking."

"You haven't changed."

"I wasn't watching where I was going, Father, that's all!"

"I see," Ellis said, making it sound like a reprimand. "Aren't you going to introduce your friend?"

She took a deep breath. "He's rather more than a friend. I'd like you to meet my fiancé, Father, Jethro Lathem. Jethro, my father, Ellis Scott."

Jethro strode forward, shaking Ellis's hand. "How do you do, sir?"

"Lathem. Of Lathem Fleets?" Ellis rapped.

"That's correct."

"I see...you've done very well for yourself the last ten years or so, Mr. Lathem. You're into pharmaceuticals and aerospace technology now as well, I believe."

"Only in a small way. The oil tankers and container ships are my main interest."

Celia's head had been snapping back and forth as she followed this exchange. Boating, Jethro had told her when she'd asked him what he did. She'd pictured yachts, perhaps a marina or a small boatyard in Maine. She croaked, "What are—"

Ellis said with a tight smile, "You're a dark horse, Celia. Why didn't you tell me you knew Mr. Lathem?"

"I—I wanted to surprise you."

"You've more than succeeded," he said drily. "And how did you meet him?"

"My yacht went aground in a storm the week before last," Jethro interposed. "Celia was on duty that night. Later, I went to Collings Cove to thank her in person."

"So that place finally did you some good, Celia," Ellis said acerbically, then turned to Jethro. "She's always refused to go around in society—I was beginning to think she'd never meet an acceptable partner."

Jethro's smile lingered possessively on Celia's flushed cheeks. "I'm glad she never did. It was love at first sight, wasn't it, darling? It took me by surprise, I know that. Of course, I can't speak for Celia."

Say something, Celia, she thought frantically. *Quit gawping like a stranded fish.* "Nothing like it has ever happened to me before," she said truthfully, forcing an adoring smile to her lips as she gazed with doe eyes at Jethro.

She'd kill him. Murder him. Slowly. Inch by inch.

Reaching up, she kissed him on the cheek, her laugh sounding utterly false. "We want to get married very soon, Father. I know that'll make you happy."

"More than happy," Ellis said. "You've done very well for yourself, Celia. My congratulations."

Jethro must be worth a mint for her father to be looking at her with such respect. Container ships. Oil tankers. How *dare* Jethro deceive her like that? "Thank you, Father," she said, and sat down. "Can I get Jethro to pour you a drink?"

Her father sank back into his chair; he'd lost more weight, she noticed with a pang of fear. "Ring for Melcher," he wheezed. "This deserves champagne."

So Jethro's absolutely filthy rich, thought Celia, and a few minutes later did her best to look like a blushing bride-to-be as Ellis raised his glass to her in a toast. Then he said to Jethro, "How soon can you get a marriage licence?"

"Why don't we settle on next Saturday for the wedding?" Jethro suggested. "Would that suit you, sir?"

"The sooner the better," Ellis said with a touch of grimness. "Phone your brother tonight, Celia, and make sure they'll be here. You'll wear white, of course?"

"If you'd like me to."

"A private ceremony here at the house. Get the best caterer, Melcher will advise you. Not too many guests, I'm not up to it." He added with a wintry smile, "I'm sure I'll still fit into my tuxedo."

He'd made a joke. A small one, but a joke, nevertheless. Sudden tears wavered in Celia's vision. Her father never joked; he had no sense of humor. But for once, she'd made him happy. Done the right thing. Been a good daughter instead of a disappointment to him. Ellis said gruffly, "No need to cry, girl."

Impulsively, she got up and hugged him, terrified of how frail he felt under his tweed jacket. "I just want you to be happy," she whispered.

"You've made a fine choice, I'm proud of you." Ellis put down his glass. "Lathem, you and I must have a chat after dinner. No need for you to be there, Celia, there'll be some business matters we'll need to discuss."

Her father had always had a feudal outlook; why should he have changed just because she was getting married? And the fact that this whole marriage was a business matter was something Celia had to keep to herself. She gulped down her champagne and refilled all three glasses, talking and laughing like a wind-up toy. Finally she said, "Father, you look tired. Why don't you have a little rest before dinner? Seven-thirty as usual?"

"Fine. Put Mr. Lathem in the west wing, Celia. Later on, I'll send Melcher up to check that everything's in order."

Her father struggled to his feet as she got up. She kissed him on his withered cheek, gave Jethro a dewy-eyed smile and led the way out of her father's suite. Jethro closed the door behind them. Without looking at him she marched to the west wing and threw open the door. Jethro's luggage was already sitting on the Indian silk carpet. Whirling to face him, she spat, "How *dare* you? Deceiving me like that, making a fool of me in front of my father—I've never been so humiliated in my life!"

He raised one brow sardonically. "The money, you mean?"

"Yes, Jethro," she said, her voice laden with sarcasm, "the money. Your money. Why didn't you tell me you were rich?"

"You didn't ask."

"Exactly how much are you worth?"

"I could buy your father fifty times over," he said lazily.

Although, she noticed, there was nothing lazy about his eyes; they were trained on her face, hard eyes that gave nothing away. She started pacing back and forth on the carpet, her hands thrust into the pockets of her linen trousers. "How you must have been laughing at me the last couple of days! Clever little Celia, hiring you to do her dirty work. Thinking she was doing you a favor. Sixty thousand dollars, a down payment for a new boat." Viciously she yanked the clip from her ponytail, shaking her hair free. "You could buy a thousand yachts and not even miss the money. A whole goldarn fleet of them!"

Jethro drawled, "You look magnificent in a rage."

She stopped dead. "Watch it, Jethro—don't push your luck. I'm so angry with you I could…I could—"

"Words failing you, Celia? You *must* be angry."

"You're enjoying this, aren't you?"

"Yeah," he said with an air of discovery, "I am."

"I'm glad someone is!" She began marching up and down again, throwing the words over her shoulder. "I'm surprised you didn't have a clause in the contract so I can't get my hands on your money. Your fortune, I should say. You'd better watch out, once we're married I'm going on the biggest spending spree in history."

He laughed. "I could buy a lot of Cessnas, honeybunch."

"Diamonds, race horses, yachts, mansions—"

"You're not the type, and that first contract was only temporary. I'll make sure the second one protects my assets."

"I'm sure you—" Again Celia stopped in her tracks,

her face stunned, as though she'd been suddenly hit on the head. There was one horribly obvious question. A question she'd been too angry to even think of, let alone ask. Her heart hammering against her rib cage, she stammered, "But why did you agree to marry me? If you don't need the money."

"I wondered when you'd get around to that."

Her lips compressed. "Why, Jethro?"

"Haven't you guessed?"

In two swift steps he closed the distance between them and pulled her the length of his body, hip to hip, breast to chest. Then he kissed her with an intensity that to her mingled horror and fury ignited her whole body to a conflagration of desire. The romance novels she used to read had often compared passion to flames, she thought feverishly, and felt herself falling into the very heart of the fire, into heat and light and the hardness of a man's body.

Impossible to resist.

She threw her arms around his neck. His hands were at her waist, her hips, his own hungers sparking her own. Then he was caressing the swell of her breast through the thin silk of her shirt, her nipple tightening in frantic response, her flesh arching to meet him. Forgetting fear or caution, she felt his erection like a throbbing in her own blood, and ached to touch his naked skin. She dragged her palm down his chest, fumbling with the first button on his shirt.

"Oh...excuse me, sir, miss...I'll come back later."

Gasping for breath, her eyes as startled as a deer's, Celia looked over her shoulder. Melcher, the butler, was about to close the door. He looked scandalized. Melcher and her great-great-grandfather, she'd often thought, would have been soulmates.

It'd be all over the house that she and Jethro were lovers.

The door snapped shut. Jethro said flatly, "He did knock, I realize that now. So, have you got your answer, Celia?"

"Answer?" she repeated blankly.

"Why I agreed to marry you?"

She flushed scarlet, pulling away from him. "We're not going to bed, Jethro! Now or after we're married. We're not!"

"Who are you trying to convince—me or you?"

She flung discretion to the wind. "You're rich as Croesus, you're handsome as all get out and sexier than twenty Hollywood movie stars. So what if my father's Ellis Scott III—don't tell me you're so desperate for sex you've got to get it by marrying a Coast Guard operator from Collings Cove. A woman who's too stupid to recognize you for what you are. You can get sex anytime you want it, Jethro Lathem. So why the *hell* would you want to get married?"

"But not sex with you, darling Celia," he said. "You're the exception that proves the rule. Other women throw themselves at me like waves on a reef. You don't do that. You're different."

She crossed her arms over her breast. If passion was a fire, then what Jethro was saying now was a glacier, chilling her to the bone. "You mean the only reason you want me is because I'm not willing?"

"I'm not Darryl! I've told you that."

"Then stop behaving like him!"

He snarled, "Did you ever respond to Darryl the way you responded to me just then?"

Her mouth a mutinous line, she muttered, "No."

Jethro raked his fingers through his hair. Then he said in a strange voice, "It didn't occur to you to lie, did it?"

"I told you before, I'm a lousy liar."

"Why don't we drop all this?" he demanded. "You saved my life that night, Celia. Now I'm doing you a favor in return. Your father's happy you're getting married. Forget the rest."

"Oh sure, just like that."

In a silky voice he said, "You're the one who asked me to marry you...or are you forgetting that?"

"I've done some stupid things in my life but that one takes the cake. My father was always telling me to think before I acted."

"Too bad you hadn't listened."

"You've got to stop kissing me," she cried.

"We're supposed to be in love, you can't have it all ways. Anyway," Jethro finished with an unpleasant smile, "I'm only earning my pay."

Her shoulders sagged. "I can't take any more of this," she said in a low voice.

"There's another reason I'm going to marry you," he said abruptly. "My life was getting in a rut...I was bored a lot of the time. Nothing like almost drowning in the North Atlantic to sharpen your mind, make you see that you need a new challenge."

"Bored," Celia repeated in a stony voice. "So I'm a new challenge, am I? Why don't you go climb an active volcano instead, Jethro? And when you get to the top, jump in."

He had the audacity to laugh. "That's not very nice of you."

"I don't feel nice! I feel homicidal."

"When you've climbed K2 and sailed solo round the

southern hemisphere, new challenges are kind of scarce on the ground.''

''Am I supposed to be complimented? Gee whiz, I'm more exciting than a killer mountain?''

''Oh, you're that all right. And about as predictable as a Himalayan blizzard.''

She hated the glint of amusement in his eye. ''I'll wear black at the wedding with a pumpkin on my head.''

''You'll look gorgeous whatever you wear.''

What she really hated about this conversation was how she understood exactly where he was coming from. Hadn't she refused to get involved with Paul because he didn't challenge her? Hadn't she left the Coast Guard job partly because she was bored? Jethro didn't bore her. Jethro was a challenge. Not that she was going to tell him that. ''I wonder how long before I bore you?'' she said sweetly. ''Three months, do you think? Or three days?''

''Time will tell, won't it?'' he said. ''And now, if I'm going to hold up my end as your fiancé, I'd better go out a buy some decent clothes. Tux for dinner?''

''Business suit,'' she said. ''Right up your alley.''

''You don't let up, do you?'' Jethro said amiably, picked up his jacket and closed the door behind him.

Celia sank down on the nearest chair. Jethro had agreed to marry her from a mixture of lust and boredom. She didn't know which word she loathed more. Oh Paul, she thought, I should have listened to you.

But today she had made her father happy. Her frail, proud father who looked so dreadfully ill. And making Ellis happy was the purpose of this whole exercise.

Wasn't it?

CHAPTER SEVEN

JETHRO got back to Fernleigh with twenty minutes to spare before dinner. He showered, shaved and dressed in his new suit, slicking down his wet hair in the mirror. Why *was* he marrying Celia? When she'd railed at him about sex, she'd been uncomfortably accurate; he'd never had any trouble finding himself a new woman. So why was he embarking on marriage with a redhead who had a temper like a shrew? A fake marriage, yeah. But still marriage.

All the gossip columns would treat it like a real marriage.

He winced away from that thought and glanced at his watch. He was late. Not the way to impress his future father-in-law. He hurried downstairs to the formal dining room, where Celia was leaning forward to help her father into the chair at the head of an enormous rosewood table. Her cleavage was exquisite; and Celia herself in a flowered blue dress with her hair in loose curls to her shoulders took his breath away. "Sorry I'm late, darling," he said, and kissed her on the mouth.

She smelled delicious; he felt the involuntary hardening of his groin, and hurriedly sat down across from her. There was an expanse of gleaming wood and a great deal of cutlery, crystal, and highly polished silverware between them. Just as well, he thought, and started up a conversation.

Dinner seemed interminable. But eventually he and Ellis were closeted with brandy in Ellis's study. Although the man looked exhausted, he'd never admit to it, thought Jethro; Ellis was every bit as stubborn and proud as his daughter. Quickly Jethro ran over his business holdings and his net worth. "I'll make a very generous settlement on Celia, of course," he said, not liking himself for the lie. "We'll see a lawyer first thing this week."

"This love affair, it's all happened very fast," Ellis said quizzically.

"Yes, sir. But we're both old enough to know our own minds."

Ellis gave the bark that passed with him for laughter. "Well, at least you're not marrying her for her money. She got burned more than once that way." He gave Jethro a level glance. "You're in love with my daughter, Jethro?"

"I love Celia, yes," Jethro said with as much conviction as he could muster. The words sounded odd on his tongue. He'd never told a woman other than his sister that he loved her. Never planned to. He was too much of a loner for that.

But there was one thing he'd learned today. Celia wasn't after him for his money. He'd watched her face when Ellis had first mentioned the Lathem Fleet. She'd been shocked, furious and humiliated. But she hadn't been the slightest bit avaricious. Not like Marliese and Elisabeth.

She couldn't have seen that newspaper article in Collings Cove. Although he didn't understand why.

He tried to pay attention, listing his various residences around the world, starting with the loft in Manhattan and ending with the Paris flat. But he didn't tell Ellis about his retreat in the mountains of Vermont. That place was his alone. The place he went to be himself, away from everyone else. He'd never taken a woman there and he wasn't about to start. No, Ellis didn't need to know about Vermont any more than Celia did.

Eventually he said, "Sir, we can continue this tomorrow, it's been a long day." He hesitated, knowing he was stepping on thin ice. "Might I ask exactly what's wrong with you? I've hated to bother Celia with too many questions, she's been so worried about you."

"I'm glad she's home," Ellis muttered, "and I'm glad you'll be looking after her from now on. She'll need a strong hand, Jethro—she's far too independent for her own good. Going round the world, buying her own plane—ridiculous! You'll have your work cut out for you." He rummaged in the pile of papers on the delicate Javanese table beside him. "It's all in here, about my illness. Take it with you and don't let Celia see it. No need for her to be fretting."

Wondering how Ellis would react if he knew Celia was embarking on a fake marriage precisely to stop her father from fretting, Jethro took the folded papers and said good night. Then he went to his wing of the house, locked the door and read the report carefully, twice over. The family doctor had called in a couple of specialists. Old timers, good enough men but not on the front line; Jethro recognized the names from his pharmaceutical connections.

For the space of ten minutes, Jethro then sat very still on his bed, thinking hard.

He could make a phone call. Ask a favor. After all, Michael Stansey owed him. Much as he himself owed his friend Dave and always would. Even after the sinking of *Starspray*.

If he hadn't gone to dinner in Iceland with the captain of one of his tankers, he wouldn't have caught the flu. No flu, no Dave at the helm, no going aground. No Celia.

He grimaced. It was difficult to imagine not knowing her.

Even more difficult to imagine not wanting her. Here and now, in his bed.

He had to make the phone call, didn't he? No matter what the outcome. He wouldn't be able to live with himself if he didn't.

Jethro's second phone call in the morning was to his Manhattan lawyer. He gave him some very succinct instructions and stressed their absolute confidentiality. There, he thought, putting down the receiver. He could now tell Ellis in good faith that Celia would never want for anything, no matter what happened to Jethro.

No matter when or how they divorced.

His third call was to his sister, who lived in the Bedford Hills outside New York with her husband and two children, and was pregnant with her third child. "Jethro," Lindy exclaimed, "how nice to hear from you."

"How are you feeling?"

"Wonderful—no more morning sickness. Where are you calling from?"

"Washington."

"You can't replace *Starspray* in Washington," she teased.

"Lindy, I'm getting married."

There were several seconds of stunned silence. "You *are*? Who to?"

"The Coast Guard operator who took the Mayday signal," he said. "Love at first sight."

"You mean you've fallen in *love*?"

He felt a flicker of irritation. "Yeah," he said. "Is that outside the realm of possibility?"

"Yes, it is," she said with sisterly frankness, "I never thought you would. Is she nice?"

"She's got chestnut hair and a temper, she's not after my money, and she pilots her own plane." Plus she has a body to die for. But he wasn't going to say that to Lindy.

"Is she pretty?"

His mouth was suddenly dry. "She's beautiful," he said.

"Different from Marliese?"

"Night and day."

"I never liked Marliese," Lindy said. "Jethro, that's wonderful news. When do I get to meet her?"

"The wedding's next Saturday, here in Washington— it's her home." Rapidly he explained about Ellis's illness and the need for haste. "But if you could come up here tomorrow, I'll tell her the two of you are going for lunch."

"You'll tell her?" Lindy repeated ironically. "Same old Jethro. She'll need a temper, won't she?"

For his own reasons, he wanted Celia out of the house on Tuesday at midday. "Sometimes she even listens to me," he said, and heard his sister's gurgle of laughter.

"I'll be there, and we'll all come to the wedding. I'm so happy for you, Jethro. We all need someone to love."

Not him. He didn't. He made a noncommittal noise, asked after his niece and nephew, rang off, and went in search of Celia. He finally located her, with the help of one of the maids, eating her breakfast under a cherry tree beside the vegetable garden. She was wearing a brief sundress, her shoulders, arms and knees bare; the sunlight caught in her hair, flickering like electricity. She was reading the paper. She hadn't seen him.

He was going to marry this woman. In less than a week. He must be out of his mind.

Suddenly, as though she'd sensed his presence, Celia looked round. "Oh. It's you."

"Good morning to you too, my dearest love."

"Can it—there's no one here to hear you."

He said with sudden urgency, "Celia, in the local paper the day after the rescue it said I was rich—you must have read it. So why were you so surprised yesterday?"

Her cheeks reddened with temper. "Why? For the simple reason that I didn't see it. Isn't that obvious?"

"A community as small as Collings Cove and the word didn't get around?"

"I came to Washington the day after *Starspray* sank," she said in a staccato voice. "By the time I got back, two fishing boats had been lost on the Grand Banks and a colleague was pregnant. There were other things to talk about than you, in other words. Besides, I'm not the slightest bit interested in your money."

"You aren't, are you?" he said slowly, and would have found it quite impossible to categorize the emotions roiling in his chest. "There's one more condition I want you to put in the contract," he added curtly. "For the duration of the marriage you won't have an affair with anyone else."

Her peal of laughter scraped his nerves like sandpaper. "Not a worry in the world. Believe me."

"Aren't you going to ask the same of me?"

"I wasn't planning on it."

He tamped down an anger whose source he didn't want to analyze. "What about the man who calls you sweetheart?"

"He doesn't exist," she said shortly.

"What do you mean?"

She looked him right in the eye. "*Sweetheart* happens

to be a term I really like. I plan on keeping it for the man I fall in love with. Who isn't you.''

His first reaction was relief there was no other man; his second, utter fury that she could dismiss him, Jethro, so cavalierly. Someone needed to teach Celia Scott a lesson. And maybe that somebody was him. ''You're going to the lawyer this morning, aren't you? See that my interests are protected, and when you're finished, bring the contract with you. I'll meet you afterward and we'll go over it.''

''Very well,'' she said.

Her laughter had vanished as if it had never been. Jethro sat down across from her and poured himself a coffee. ''Where's the business section?'' he said.

The business section. What else would he want, Celia wondered. The funnies? But as Jethro sat down across from her, his big body was speckled with shadows from the leaves, and the muscles moved in his forearm as he reached for the paper. She wanted to jump him. At nine in the morning, she wanted to throw herself on top of him and kiss him senseless. ''Oh...oh sure,'' she muttered, and thrust a bundle of papers at him.

''What's the matter?''

''I—I've been trying to work on a guest list,'' she stuttered. ''I don't even know where your parents live.''

''My father's dead.''

His face was shuttered. ''When did he die?''

''You don't need—''

''Jethro, we're getting married on Saturday, and I don't know the first thing about you!'' Except that when you kiss me, I fall apart at the seams.

''My mother left my father when I was seven. After a series of highly publicized affairs, she married a French count who lives in a chateau on the Loire, and I haven't

seen her since. My father died when I was nineteen—
that's when I took over the business. I have one sister,
Lindy, five years younger than me. She lives in the
Bedford Hills and she's happily married to a lawyer who
has no ambitions beyond a country practice. Two kids and
a third on the way.''

Apart from the sister, there were plenty of gaps in that
little recital, thought Celia. It would be interesting to fill
them in. ''I don't even know how old you are.''

''Thirty-seven. And you?''

''Twenty-seven.'' Her sense of humor getting the better
of her, she said with a disarming smile, ''This whole process is nuts, isn't it?''

''That's one word for it.... I like your dress.''

Hadn't she chosen it with him in mind? ''I'll change
before I go to the lawyer. Which I'd better do right now
so I'll have lots of time.'' After giving him the address
and the time of her appointment, she said, ''See you
later,'' and hurried toward the house. She wasn't retreat-
ing so she wouldn't grab the man and make love to him
on the grass, of course she wasn't. She had to visit her
father and change her clothes and make sure all her notes
were in order.

No sex. She'd get the lawyer to put that in capital letters. At the top of every page.

Celia arrived outside the brick facade of Wilkins,
Chesterton and Hawthorne fifteen minutes early. She ran
across the street to the elegant mall where she'd bought
the suit she was wearing, and found a seat in the little
coffee shop. She'd added cream to her cup and was just
taking out her notes when a man's voice said, ''Celia!
What a pleasant surprise.''

She stuffed the papers back in her bag. ''Darryl...!''

He kissed her open mouth. "I didn't know you were back in town."

She pulled her head back, subduing the urge to wipe her lips. "I came back yesterday. To get married," she said.

His smile was wiped from his face, leaving his pale gray eyes cold as a winter sky. "Married? Who's the lucky guy?"

"Jethro Lathem. Of Lathem Fleets."

"You're having me on! Lathem? He's a confirmed bachelor."

"We met in Newfoundland and we fell in love," she said limpidly. "Just like in the movies."

The overhead lights shone on her cheek. "Looks like he beat you into submission," Darryl sneered.

"It was you who tried to do that," she retorted. The last evening she'd spent with Darryl, he'd hit her, his diamond signet ring grazing her cheek.

Would she ever forget that disastrous evening? She'd just graduated from the Coast Guard college, a ceremony that had meant more to her than her degree from Harvard. She and her colleagues were going on a beach party, and then Darryl showed up. He was on vacation, he said; he'd kept her address from her last Christmas card.

She was pleased to see him. Darryl was a familiar face from home; she'd dated him a few times, with her father's full approval, in her late teens.

Friendlier to him than was perhaps wise, Celia invited him to the party, where the beer and wine flowed like water. Afterward, Darryl took her back to her apartment. His good night kiss seemed like an extension of the party. But it quickly turned into something more demanding, and her resistance only excited Darryl. He started tearing at her clothes, his hands all over her, his kisses suffocating her; in true panic, she'd wrenched free and screamed, whereupon he'd slapped her hard on the face. Luckily her friend across the hall had also returned from the beach, and had come to her rescue....

With a start, Celia came back to the present. But something must have shown on her face. "Come on, Celia," Darryl said, "that was a long time ago, water under the bridge." He leaned forward confidentially. "You'd be making a big mistake to marry Lathem...he's had a string of affairs and they aren't likely to stop. Not with the kind of money he has. He pays the gal off when he's done with her and goes on to the next one. Is that what you want?"

Celia pushed her cup away. Jealousy was a disagreeable emotion, piercing as needles and oddly humiliating. Was it true that to Jethro she was just the latest in a succession of women, all of them willing except her? Jethro wasn't beating her into submission, she thought unhappily. He was kissing her into submission instead. So, in a way, she was just like the rest.

She'd been silent too long. Darryl said, "Don't do it, Celia. I'd hate for you to make a mistake like that."

"Because you're on the lookout for a rich wife?" she flashed, and saw his face change.

"Because I never really fell out of love with you.... I know I blew it after that party, just give me the chance to show you I've changed."

He was a good-looking man, she thought dispassionately, although there were already marks of dissipation under his eyes and he'd put on weight. "I'm marrying Jethro on Saturday," she said coldly.

"What's the big rush? You pregnant?"

"Darryl, my father's dying!"

"Ahh...Lathem's chance to add to his holdings—your inheritance won't be anything to sneeze at. He's utterly ruthless, of course. Ask any of his business acquaintances. Or his lovers. If you're going to see your lawyer to try and protect yourself, forget it.''

Furious that Darryl had guessed her destination, she said, hoping she sounded more convincing than she felt, "I love Jethro. And that's all that matters.''

He took her by the wrist; she'd forgotten how strong he could be. "Lathem doesn't know the meaning of the word. You're making a bad mistake, Celia, I'd suggest you do some hard thinking between now and Saturday. Wilkins is a good lawyer, no question of that. But the sharks Lathem employs could gobble up his firm for a midnight snack and spit it out before breakfast.''

Celia didn't want to hear any more. She tried to tug free, feeling his fingers tighten with momentary cruelty before he released her. "Goodbye, Darryl,'' she said, and signaled for her bill. She paid and hurried outside, rubbing at her wrist. Darryl was in no way objective, and he'd always had a mean streak. But everything he'd said about Jethro had lodged itself in her brain. Ruthless. Acquisitive. A womanizer.

She truly didn't believe Jethro was after her money. No, that wasn't the problem. And his ruthlessness she'd recognized from the first moment she'd seen him. But how she hated the thought of him in another woman's arms!

And how was that for illogical thinking when she was so adamant against finding herself anywhere near Jethro's arms?

CHAPTER EIGHT

WHEN Celia left the lawyer's office an hour and a half later, her brain was whirling. Mr. Wilkins was too old and too experienced to show any surprise at the type of contract she'd wanted. But he'd certainly made sure he was protecting her interests as well as Jethro's, a process that had somehow confirmed all Darryl's nasty insinuations. So when she emerged on the sidewalk, she had to brace herself as she saw that Jethro was waiting for her.

He looked devastatingly handsome in a tailored suit, his hair ruffled by the breeze. Although he was clean-shaven, and although the scrape on his jaw was healing over, he still looked like a man it would be dangerous to cross. He said softly, "Every time I see you, you look different."

Her chocolate brown designer suit had a straight skirt with a narrow jacket over a tawny silk shirt; gold necklaces looped her throat. It was a sophisticated outfit that she knew she wore well. She said, the words falling from her lips without thought or volition, "If I went to bed with you tonight, would you call off the wedding?"

He went very still. "No."

"But you'd be getting what you wanted. Without marriage."

"I said no, Celia. Anyway, what about your father?"

She let out her breath in a long sigh, her fingers tightening on the stiff envelope of papers she was carrying. "My father. Of course," she said tonelessly. "This is nothing to do with us and everything to do with him, why do I keep forgetting that?"

"I've booked a table at Lamartine's. Let's go."

The last thing she wanted was to sit across from Jethro in a restaurant frequented by cronies of her father's. *You can do it, Celia*, she thought, *all you have to do is act your head off*. She tucked her arm in Jethro's sleeve, pouting at him as they set off down the street. "The best restaurant in town? Honey, I'm flattered."

"Let's add one more codicil to this famous contract," Jethro grated. "I won't call you sweetheart if you don't call me honey."

"It's a done deal."

"Good. If you were so rebellious when you were younger, why didn't you fall into bed with every man who asked you?"

She said pithily, "You'd make a damned good prosecutor—you specialize in the question from left field, the curve ball no one expects." Her brow crinkled. "I don't know why! Too fastidious, maybe? Or else I kept waiting for fireworks that didn't happen."

"We go off like flares when we're within ten feet of each other," he said grimly.

"Is it like that with all your other women?" she blurted.

"How many woman do you think I've had?"

"You've got a reputation as a womanizer."

"Gutter press."

"So answer the question, Jethro."

After a fractional hesitation, he said, "I have never felt with any other woman remotely the way I feel with you."

"Oh," said Celia, her heart unaccountably lighter.

He was frowning. "So you're saying you stayed away from men because you were too fussy?"

"Do you have to make it so obvious you disbelieve me?"

"You have to admit it's hard to believe."

Celia said, without stopping to think, "I may have been only five when my mother died, but I knew my parents were deeply in love. I guess way back then I must have decided I wouldn't settle for less."

Jethro stopped dead in the middle of the sidewalk. "Are you saying you're in love with me?"

"Of course not!"

"Then why did you look ready to eat me for breakfast this morning under the cherry tree?"

"Not much escapes you, does it?" she seethed. "Call it chemistry. Hormones. Lust. Whatever you like. Just don't call it love."

"Love isn't in the contract, Celia. Not for me."

"Nor for me! It doesn't have to be for either one of us." Upset in a way that made no sense, she saw with huge relief the striped awnings of the restaurant just ahead of them. She said, "I hope you reserved a table by the courtyard."

He had. Celia chose a mandarin almond salad and crepes and sipped on the excellent wine Jethro had selected. Then he said, "Let me see this famous contract."

She watched as he read it, seeing anew the formidable strength of his jawline, the jut of his cheekbones, the way his hair fell forward across his forehead. Even his ears were sexy, she thought uneasily. She'd never noticed Darryl's ears. Or Paul's.

As the waiter brought their salads, Jethro looked up and said pleasantly to the young man, "Would you mind witnessing our signatures?"

Jethro signed at the bottom of the page and passed his gold pen to Celia. Her throat suddenly dry, she too signed, then watched the waiter add his name and leave their table. His blue eyes mocking, Jethro passed her back the document. "All yours," he said. "As am I. Temporarily."

"Temporary is what this is about."

"As you're always so quick to remind me." Jethro drew a small velvet-covered box from his pocket. "Nevertheless, I hope you like this."

"I don't want a ring!"

His mouth hardened. "Your father will expect it."

It always came back to Ellis, she thought in momentary despair. "Then I'll give it back to you afterward."

"Let's deal with right now first, okay?" Jethro snarled.

He didn't look like a man about to become formally engaged. He looked as though he'd like to throttle her. Awkwardly, Celia opened the box, then gave an involuntary gasp of delight. The ring was a solitaire, the stone a rare yellow diamond, almost the hue of amber. "It's beautiful...as though you knew just what I'd like."

He said tersely, "It reminded me of the way sunlight catches in your hair."

Her throat closed with emotion. "That's a beautiful thing to say...thank you, Jethro," she whispered. The ring was shimmering in the box because her eyes were suddenly full of tears; she wanted to lay her head on the tablecloth and weep. How could a gift that was motivated by falsity feel so right, so perfect?

"Celia, don't—I can't stand to see you cry."

She dabbed at her eyes with her napkin. "Then I won't."

"Here, give me your hand." But as she stretched out her left wrist, he rapped, "Who did that to you?"

The marks of Darryl's fingers were imprinted on her skin. "I—I bumped into Darryl before my appointment.

He...was trying to persuade me that I shouldn't marry you."

"You just happened to meet him."

"That's right," she said, refusing to drop her gaze.

"If he as much as lays a finger on you again, I'll have his hide for a doormat."

"If I didn't know better, I'd say you were jealous."

He slipped the ring on her finger, his steel-blue eyes blazing. "You're mine, Celia. Mine. Don't you forget it."

"For three months only. Don't you forget that!"

He raised her fingers to his lips and kissed them one by one, his eyes fastened on her face. She could no more have controlled her shudder of response than she could have stopped breathing.

She wanted him. And she was terrified of him.

Terrified of what he made her feel.

"But aren't you the tiniest bit scared of him?"

Celia smiled at Jethro's sister. She and Lindy McKelvie had met an hour ago, had been talking with the ease of old friends ever since, and were now eating lunch in a charming colonial restaurant in Georgetown; the diamond flashed on Celia's finger as she buttered her roll. "If I am, I certainly wouldn't tell him so," she said lightly.

"He's always been my big brother. He looked after me when I was little and he's so different from me...." Lindy poked at her salad, her piquant face troubled under its clustered dark curls. "I guess I've never really understood him."

Welcome to the club, thought Celia. She liked Jethro's sister, who seemed genuinely happy that her brother was getting married. "He told me your mother left when you were very young."

"Did he? He doesn't like talking about our parents."

"You've got that right."

"Dad was an awful man." Lindy shivered. "Jethro kept me safe, shielded me when my father was drinking.... I suppose over the years my brother became my surrogate father. It's a terrible thing, Celia, to be relieved when one of your parents dies."

So Jethro's father had been a man of violence. Celia covered Lindy's hand with her own. "Don't talk about it if it upsets you."

"Dad was mean to Jethro. I sometimes think he hated him, his very own son." She looked up, her blue eyes open where Jethro's were guarded. "I've worried about Jethro the last few years. I've been afraid he'd never allow himself to fall in love like everyone else, and be happy. I'm so glad he's met you, Celia—I know we don't know each other very well, but I think you're perfect for him."

With a sharp prickle of shame Celia remembered the contract she and Jethro had signed yesterday, with its carefully worded clauses about divorce. One thing to deceive her father, who wouldn't be here to know how false the marriage had been. Quite another to deceive Lindy, with her sweet smile: Lindy, who loved her brother. "We argue a lot," Celia confessed.

Lindy grinned. "He told me you had a temper. You do realize there'll be women who'll want to put arsenic in your soup when they hear he's getting married?"

"I gathered as much."

"But you don't need to worry—he never loved any of them," Lindy said with uncharacteristic fierceness. "I know that for a fact."

He doesn't love me.

Celia speared a piece of zucchini with vicious accuracy and said, abandoning truth, "I'm looking forward to seeing Jethro's Manhattan place."

"The loft? It's wonderful, I love going there. So much less formal than the Paris apartment." She chuckled. "More formal than the lodge in Vermont, though. I'm sure he'll take you there.... It's his retreat, the place he goes when he wants to get away from work and all the people who only want something from him."

Celia's lashes flickered; she was one of those people. But this was the first she'd heard about a lodge in Vermont; she was sure Jethro hadn't mentioned it.

"It's in the Green Mountains," Lindy said dreamily. "There's a little stream runs by the house, and the trees are beautiful no matter what the time of year.... You'll like it there."

If it was Jethro's retreat, she wouldn't get the chance. With some determination Celia changed the subject to her unsuccessful hunt for a wedding dress. Lindy's face lit up. "I know a couple of wonderful boutiques not far from here. We could go after lunch if you liked."

But although they found some very attractive gowns, Celia knew none of them was quite right. She said goodbye to Lindy a little after four and went home. Her father was resting, Melcher said, and Mr. Lathem was out. After telling the butler she was going for an hour's run, she changed into her Spandex shorts and a top and set out, jogging down the broad avenue toward the heart of Washington, where she looped around Capitol Hill, then headed west down the Mall. Her stride settled into an easy rhythm.

She loved running the length of the Mall, past the Smithsonian Institutions. The Hirshhorn sculpture garden was still full of tourists, the sound of traffic muted by its plashing fountain. The flags around the Washington monument snapped in the breeze; paddleboats dotted the waters of the Tidal Basin. She could have gone north up

17th Street, toward home. But she wasn't ready to go home yet.

Keeping to the sidewalk that circled the basin, she passed the cherry trees whose blossoming was a time of festivals and renewal. Her father wouldn't be here in the spring to see their clustered pink and white petals, she thought, and felt her throat tighten with tears. She had to marry Jethro. She had to. Her father was more important than her own feelings; for three months she could put up with anything.

If only it were that simple...unfortunately, another huge part of her knew she should never have started this deception. She should have realized how many other people would be involved, people like Lindy who dearly loved Jethro and would be devastated when the divorce went through so soon after the wedding.

It was the story of her life, Celia thought moodily, heading north toward the Lincoln Memorial. Act first, think later and to heck with the consequences.

She looped around the lake in the Constitution Gardens, where the dahlias were starting to look bedraggled. Feeling her body begin to tire and sweat beginning to dampen her top, she dodged through the pedestrians on 23rd Street. A vendor was selling hot dogs on the corner. Her mouth watering, she kept running. She'd surpassed herself today. Nearly two hours. Although she'd pay for it tomorrow, it had felt good to reclaim parts of the city that was her home; and better still to be out of the house.

She couldn't run forever. Sooner or later she had to go home and see her father and Jethro, pick up the tangled strands of a deception for which she was wholly responsible.

Breathing deeply, she paced herself and before she reached the iron gates of Fernleigh, slowed to a walk.

Once she was in the grounds, Celia circled to the back door, stretching out her calf muscles against the stone wall, checking her pulse rate. Then the door burst open and Jethro demanded, "Where the hell have you been?"

Her fragile peace evaporated. She grabbed her left heel, bringing it up to her buttock. "Buying a wedding dress, can't you tell?"

He seized her by the elbows, his eyes raking her sweat-damp hair and heaving breasts. "You told Melcher you'd be gone an hour."

"I changed my mind."

"This isn't Collings Cove, Celia—this is the big city. Do you want your father worrying about you? Being afraid you've been kidnapped or mugged?"

"Jethro," Celia said through gritted teeth, "you sound just like him. Don't you dare try and control me—I won't have it! I'm twenty-seven years old, I'm streetwise and I'm not late for dinner. So lay off."

"There's something you're not getting," Jethro said with menacing clarity. "I don't like being told what to do."

"Then quit telling me what to do," she flared. "If I didn't know better, I'd think you were the one who was worried."

A muscle twitched in his jaw. "Would you?" he said. "Don't overestimate yourself."

She hated it when he used that tone of voice; hated it, too, that mere words could hurt her so deeply. "Pardon me...I'm only your fiancée, after all."

"You have to be the most infuriating woman I've come across in my whole life," Jethro said, and kissed her hard on the mouth. His hands roaming her hips, he muttered against her lips, "You taste of salt and those shorts should be outlawed."

It's you who should be outlawed, she thought, and pushed against his chest. "I need to shower before dinner and see my father. Let go!"

"He's resting."

She frowned up at Jethro. "So? I'm his daughter—if he's asleep, I'll leave."

"Let him be...you'll see him at dinner."

"Fine," she said and yanked the door open. Jethro made no move to stop her, she noticed; and on impulse ran upstairs to her father's suite rather than her own. Tapping gently on the door, she let herself in. Ellis was sitting by the window, a magazine open in his lap. "Ah...Celia."

"I just wanted to check on you before dinner," she said lamely.

He looked at her attire with displeasure. "I wish you wouldn't run through the streets dressed like that. You shouldn't be out jogging at all."

"I just went around the Mall...I was quite safe."

"I'm glad you're marrying Jethro—he'll keep you in line."

She said with a touch of desperation, "Surely keeping me in line isn't what marriage is all about?"

"You haven't changed one bit, Celia—this city's a dangerous place and you haven't even taken off the ring Jethro gave you—you're asking for trouble."

She said in a low voice, "I have changed. Five years ago I wouldn't have been here with you, Father. I'm trying...I'm really trying."

For a moment Ellis looked at a loss for words. Then he said stiffly, "Well. I suppose so. Now that you're here, I might as well tell you I'll be keeping to my room a fair bit this week. Resting up for the big day."

"Are you feeling worse?" she asked in quick alarm.

"I said I'd be resting, Celia."

She knew it was useless to push him. Briefly she pressed her cheek to his wrinkled face. "Why don't you have dinner served here rather than sit for so long in the dining room?"

"Jethro will be in New York tomorrow until late Friday—business matters—as I'm sure you know. So I'll be taking my meals in here while he's gone."

She hadn't known. Three days without him, she thought with enormous relief; a relief that almost masked the hurt that her father wasn't offering to share his meals with her. "Just look after yourself," she pleaded, patted him on the sleeve and left him alone.

In her own rooms, she showered and dressed in pale cream trousers with a matching angora sweater, leaving her hair loose. By the time she hurried downstairs, her father and Jethro were already in the dining room; instantly she knew they'd been saying something not for her ears. She paused, looking from one to the other of them. "Okay—what's up?"

Ellis said impatiently, "We were discussing arrangements for the wedding."

He was lying; she knew it. "In that case, I'd better hurry up and find a dress," she said. "I'd hate to have to wear my jogging shorts."

Her father sat down at the head of the table. "I was asking Jethro where you'd be spending your honeymoon."

Jethro said, "We hadn't yet discussed—"

"No honeymoon," Celia interrupted, panic-stricken. "Not while you're ill, Father."

"I want you to take at least three or four days," Ellis announced.

"I've got a luxury cruiser in the Caribbean," Jethro

drawled. "If you prefer, we could take the Concorde to Paris....or is there some other romantic hideaway you'd like, darling?"

You know what I'd like, she thought. I'd like to throw the nearest plate at you. "But your business," she said artlessly, "you've been away so much lately."

"Oh, didn't I tell you? I'm taking the shuttle to the city tomorrow until Friday. A honeymoon's no problem—just name the place."

She was caught. Well and truly caught. "In that case, I'd love to go to your lodge in the Green Mountains."

Jethro's eyes narrowed. "How—you had lunch with Lindy today, didn't you?"

Finally she could say something truthful. "I really like her. And she painted such a glowing picture of the lodge."

"Then the lodge it'll be."

She'd made him agree to something he didn't want to do: no small achievement. But the result was that she'd be spending three days alone with him in the middle of the woods. Oh God, thought Celia, sitting down at the table, will I ever learn to think before I open my mouth? "We'll come back on Tuesday, Father, and no arguments."

"Very well," said Ellis.

At least Jethro would be away until Friday. Three days without him.

Three months as his wife.

She could do it. Of course she could.

CHAPTER NINE

CELIA and Jethro were to be married at eleven on Saturday morning, to give them time to get to the lodge before dark. Celia was dressed and ready by eighteen minutes after ten. She didn't want to sit down and crease her skirt and she couldn't bear watching her bedside clock tick off the minutes with such agonizing slowness. So she crept out of her room, feeling like a thief in her own house, and tapped on her father's door.

She'd seen very little of him all week; he'd kept himself sequestered in his rooms and hadn't encouraged her to visit him. She could only conclude he was feeling worse. No time to waste, she'd thought on Thursday when she'd finally found the perfect wedding dress; Saturday was none too soon for the ceremony.

When she walked in, Ellis was struggling with the clips on his black bowtie. He saw Celia in the mirror; his mouth dropped open and his tie fell onto the mahogany bureau. He said faintly, "Marian..."

Marian was her mother's name. Celia's heart skipped a beat. She faltered, "Do I look like her?"

"In that suit...your hair...yes, you look like her." He straightened to his full height, years somehow seeming to drop from his age. "She was the most beautiful woman I ever saw."

Celia's throat tightened with emotion. "You know what? I still miss her. After all this time."

Ellis said gruffly, fumbling to pick up his tie, "I didn't

112

do well by you after Marian died, Celia. I couldn't bear to talk about her, so I didn't allow you to talk about her, either. That was wrong of me.''

Celia stepped closer, seeing her own reflection in her father's mirror. Taking her courage in her hands, she said, ''I thought you didn't love me any more.''

An old pain flickered across Ellis's face. ''I loved you. I just didn't know how to tell you. And that was wrong of me, too.''

''Do you love me now?'' Celia whispered.

He turned so he was facing her; because she was wearing high heels, her eyes were level with his. ''Yes,'' he said. ''Very much. Why else do you think I keep trying to keep you safe?''

So she'd been right. Love had always been the motive behind his protectiveness and control. ''I can keep myself safe,'' she said steadfastly, ''and I'll always be here for you. Because I love you, too.''

And suddenly she was in his arms, weeping as though her heart would break, feeling him hold her close. He muttered against her cheek, ''Marian was like you in so many ways. She never let me get away with anything...I wanted her to fly to Chicago, but she loved being on the road. We had a huge argument before she left. She took the car...and died in a collision with a drunk driver. I'd give my soul to take away that argument.''

''So every time I rebelled, you had to insist you got your own way,'' Celia said, raising her head. ''That makes such sense to me now...what else could you have done?''

''But it pushed you away. I could see that. Yet I couldn't stop—the more you rebelled, the more I tried to control you.''

''If I wasn't marrying Jethro,'' Celia said, smiling

through her tears, "we might never have had this conversation."

"Humph," said Ellis. "He'll make you a good husband, Celia. He's a man for the long haul."

With a huge effort she kept her gaze level. "I'm glad you like him."

"Far superior to Darryl Coates. I know I encouraged you to date Darryl all those years ago—I'm very glad it didn't go anywhere. His recent divorce, all the dirty linen dragged through the courts...a disgrace."

Divorce. Celia dropped her eyes, taking the tie from her father's fingers and carefully adjusting the clips round the collar of his starched shirt. Ellis added, "Darryl came to see me a couple of days ago. Did his best to stop your marriage by telling me a lot of scurrilous gossip about Jethro's past. I told him Jethro was ten times the man he'd ever be, and that you were very much in love with your future husband." He directed a self-satisfied smile at the mirror. "Sent him packing."

A small part of her had to admire Darryl's nerve. "I wish I'd been a fly on the wall," she said.

Her father's laugh creaked like an unoiled hinge. "He left in rather a hurry."

Grinning at him in the mirror, she said, "I'd better go and fix my face—my mascara's all smeared. So much for waterproof." Impulsively she hugged Ellis again. "Thanks, Dad," she gulped. "Don't you ever forget I love you."

Ellis cleared his throat. "We'll talk more about your mother when you're back from your honeymoon," he said. "If you like."

"I'd really like that."

Knowing she had to get out of here before she started bawling like a baby, Celia hurried down the hall to her room and repaired the damage to her makeup. It was now five to eleven. She took a couple of deep breaths and picked up the sheaf of pale gold lilies she'd chosen instead of a more traditional bouquet; they went beautifully with the ring Jethro had given her.

Her father had never stopped loving her, she thought in pure happiness. And indirectly, of course, she had Jethro to thank for that revelation.

In marrying Jethro, she was doing the wrong thing for all the right reasons. Or was it the other way round?

She wasn't sure. But she felt oddly calm as she left her room and began to descend the stairs. Nothing like a good cry to settle the nerves, she thought ruefully; and wondered if Jethro would like her dress.

Jethro was already waiting in the living room, with its high ceilings and impressive collection of nineteenth-century American antiques. At least there weren't any dour-faced ancestors on the walls. He tried to pay attention to Celia's brother Cyril, who was as conservative and correct as Celia was quick-witted and vibrant. Cyril's wife was self-effacing, while his two daughters were looking rather enviously at Lindy's more boisterous children.

Jethro was glad Lindy and her husband Doug were here; although his sister's open delight in his prospective wedding made him highly uncomfortable. One minute to eleven. He only hoped Celia wouldn't be late; every nerve in his body already felt stretched taut as a bow. One occasion when he didn't have to act, he thought grimly. He felt and probably looked exactly like the typical nervous bridegroom.

Was Celia nervous? What if at the last minute she decided she couldn't go through with it?

Then the chamber musicians grouped by the tall windows struck up a wedding processional. The clergyman took his place in front of Jethro; Dave, patting his pocket to make sure he had the ring, came to stand next to Jethro, giving him a comradely wink. Lindy, who looked very pretty in her yellow gown, smiled at him lovingly from his other side. He was getting married, he thought blankly. Married.

It had never been among his plans to embark on matrimony. Especially to a woman he scarcely knew, who possessed the unique and very irritating ability to get under his skin.

Slowly he turned around. Celia was walking toward him, her hand on her father's sleeve. Her head was held high; she looked calm and composed and so startlingly beautiful that his heart gave a great thud in his chest and he felt a primitive rush of possessiveness.

She was wearing a pure white suit with a long slim skirt slit to the knee on one side, and a jacket that hugged her body; its neckline plunged in a sharp V, the raised collar cupping her slender throat and emphasizing in its severity the soft glow of her skin and the delicacy of her collarbones. Her hair was pulled away from her face and knotted on the back of her head. She was carrying three lilies, as simple and sensuous as her dress.

It was as though he'd never seen her before.

And then she smiled at him, a grave smile that he sensed was at some level unsure of itself. In a flash of admiration for her courage, he smiled back, and watched as her own smile deepened.

She was so incredibly beautiful. So elegant, so devastatingly desirable.

So complicated and hot-tempered and independent.

He was going to marry her.

He felt the same rush of adrenaline that had taken him

to the peak of K2; that had kept him at the wheel of *Starspray* in thirty-foot seas. A challenge, he thought. A challenge unlike any other in his life.

Her father patted her hand and stood to one side. Celia directed her gaze at the clergyman, and from a long way away Jethro heard the words, "Dearly beloved, we are gathered…"

He made all the appropriate responses; Celia's voice sounded as clear and calm as it had on *Starspray*'s radio in the middle of a storm. Her second name was Marian. He'd never asked her full name.

There was a lot he'd never asked her.

He promised to love her and keep her, to honor and cherish her; and such was the power of the words that Jethro forgot this was a sham, a fake marriage that would end in divorce. His own voice sounded deep and sure of itself; the challenge was real.

He'd bought a narrow gold band the same day he'd found the yellow diamond; as he slipped it on her finger, he noticed her hand was cold, and trembling slightly. He pressed it gently, trying to reassure her; then stood very still as, her tongue caught in her teeth, she fumbled to push a wider band on his finger.

"I now declare you man and wife…"

He'd done it. He'd married Celia Marian Scott. She was his wife. Until death do us part, Jethro thought, and was suddenly aware of how hard his heart was beating.

"…may kiss the bride."

Jethro took Celia in his arms, kissing her with a swift, passionate intensity. Her cheeks were flushed when he released her; Lindy, he noticed distantly, had tears hanging on her lashes. Then Lindy and Dave were hugging them both, Cyril had embarked on what sounded like a presidential address, and Ellis was patting him on the back.

Jethro's nephew Stephen, aged five, tugged at his trouser leg. "Uncle Jethro, are you her husband now?"

"That's right, Stevie. You can call her Aunt Celia."

"D'you love her like Dad loves Mum?"

"Yes, I do," he said, keeping his gaze very steady.

"She's real pretty."

Jethro looked up, straight into Celia's face; he said, "She's the most beautiful woman I've ever seen."

Tears flooded Celia's eyes. She whispered, "That's what my father said about my mother...he loved her so much."

And what was he supposed to say to that? Board meetings with millions at stake, business rivals, takeovers, he could handle them all with consummate skill; yet right now he was speechless. "You...look very different than the first time I saw you."

Her smile was more natural. "That was the object."

Briefly they were isolated; everyone else seemed to be indulging in an orgy of hugging. Celia said in a rush, "Half an hour before the wedding Dad and I had the best talk we've ever had in my life—all about my mother and why he was so overly protective of me. He really loves me, Jethro—he always has."

Why should two tears clinging to a woman's lashes make his bones melt in his body? "I'm glad," Jethro said hoarsely.

"So this was all worthwhile," she finished with a radiant smile. "I've made him happy. I knew all along I was doing it for him and I was right."

Doing it for her father. Nothing to do with him, Jethro.

The clergyman suddenly reappeared, edging them both toward a walnut Duncan Phyfe table to sign the official papers that legally made them man and wife; and with a thud Jethro came all the way back to reality. Last Monday he and Celia had signed an equally legal contract about separation and divorce.

There was nothing real about this marriage. It was fake from start to finish and he'd damn well better remember it.

It was all for the benefit of Ellis Scott. Celia had been telling the truth a moment ago. He, Jethro, was the means to an end. No more, no less.

She'd used him. But she'd been honest about it from the start, and he, after all, had agreed to be used.

He got up from the table. His gut felt like a lump of lead in his belly. Dave said speculatively, "You okay?"

Act, Jethro. Isn't that what he'd told Celia to do at the airport the day they'd arrived here? "Sure," he said and put his arm round his wife's waist. "She's taken my breath away."

"She's much prettier than *Starspray*," said Dave with a grin on his ruddy face, and bent to sign the register.

Jethro could feel the tension in Celia's body through all his nerves; stroking her hip, he said, "You don't know how happy you've made me today, darling."

Her lips compressed; she was quite intelligent enough to pick up the ambiguity of his statement. "I'm sure in the next couple of months, you'll figure out a way to tell me."

There was an edge to her voice. Good, he thought. So you're not totally immune. "I can't wait for us to be alone," he murmured, and let his lips drift down the slender line of her throat. She smelled delicious; with a fierce stab of mingled lust and power, he felt her quiver to his touch.

By this evening, they'd be alone at the lodge. Alone

and together. He'd be with Celia in the one place in the world he'd always kept strictly for himself; and how cleverly—in front of her father—she'd manipulated him into taking her there!

He'd never taken any of his lovers to the lodge. It was one of his unbreakable rules. The other was never to get involved with a woman beyond certain scrupulously defined boundaries.

He was doing a lousy job of keeping both those rules.

And quite suddenly his strategy for his honeymoon dropped neatly into his mind. Yeah, he thought, turning the plan around in his head, that'll show her. Provided I can stick with it. He said easily, "Champagne's called for, don't you think, my love?"

By the time they reached the lodge in the Green Mountains, dusk was falling and every nerve in Celia's body felt as though it were pulled unbearably tight. They'd flown from Washington to Burlington in Jethro's private jet and picked up a car there, a sleek black Maserati. Then they'd driven east. Not a hitch in any of the arrangements. Of course not. She'd married Jethro Lathem, of Lathem Fleets.

The narrow dirt road, overhung with huge maples, turned a sharp corner then opened into an expanse of grass edged with a stone wall and more trees. The lodge was cedar-shingled, set so artfully among pines and birches that it looked as though it had always been there. A soft gold light shone through the tall windows, infinitely welcoming. For a painful moment whose intensity knocked her off balance, Celia wished she was here with a man she truly loved—what a heavenly place for a real honeymoon.

She smothered this sharp regret as Jethro said formally,

"A couple in the village look after the place for me. I asked them to put the heat on and leave food ready for us."

It was the first time he'd spoken in the last hour. As though, she thought bitterly, now that they were alone, there was no need to keep up any pretense. So what was he going to do? Fall on her as soon as they were through the door?

No sex. She climbed out of the car, stretching her limbs. To her left, a brook chuckled and gurgled; otherwise the silence was complete. She should have opted for the luxury cruiser or a weekend in Paris, rather than this isolated wilderness lodge with a man who was a stranger to her. She glanced up at him. His strongly chiselled features, his hair and deep-set eyes almost black in the fading light...what did she really know about him?

She knew that every time he kissed her, she turned into a woman she'd never known existed: a passionate woman who forgot all restraint in her fierce hunger for him.

She knew something else. A large part of her—the reckless Celia her father so deplored—wanted to make love to Jethro this weekend regardless of the consequences. The other part—the woman of twenty-seven who had learned that the consequences of all her actions landed squarely on her own shoulders—wanted to run a mile from him.

If she made love to him, thereby breaking one clause of the contract, did that render the rest of it invalid? She should have asked the lawyer that all-important question, she thought unhappily, and followed Jethro up the slate path to the front door. He unlocked it and ushered her in ahead of him.

She said spontaneously, "It's lovely, Jethro." The soaring cathedral ceiling and sleeping loft, an immense stone fireplace with laden bookshelves on either side, an array of colorful woven rugs: unquestionably a man's space. Yet she felt instantly at home.

For some reason this terrified her. Jethro said casually, "Let's eat, shall we? I'll check out the refrigerator, Greta usually leaves a note. The main bathroom's down the hall, Celia; there's another one upstairs. Make yourself at home."

Jethro make love to her? He was more interested in dinner than in his new wife. Nor, now that she thought about it, had he as much as laid a finger on her ever since they'd left Mason and the limo at the airport in Washington.

Celia marched down the hall. The bathroom had a Jacuzzi, piles of thick blue towels and a mirror that showed a woman with wide, frightened eyes. She was still wearing her going-away outfit, a tailored teal-blue coat over a simple sleeveless dress; her wedding ring and the yellow diamond felt funny on her finger.

Remember your father, she told herself. Remember that when he saw you in your wedding dress, the silence of years was broken. That's what this is all about.

She replenished her lipstick, dabbed on more perfume and went back to the kitchen. "The cutlery's in the drawer by the sink," Jethro said, "do you mind setting the table?"

"Not at all," she said politely. "What's for dinner?"

"I'll bake potatoes in the microwave and broil a couple of filets."

Twenty minutes later they were sitting down to eat. The food, while delicious, was wasted on Celia; throughout the meal Jethro talked wittily and intelligently about any number of things, none of which was related to their marriage, their honeymoon or their emotions. Afterward she helped him clean up the kitchen. As he was loading the dishwasher, he remarked, "I thought you'd probably want to sleep in the loft—there's a balcony that overlooks the trees, it's a pleasant place to read when the sun's out. I'll sleep downstairs."

The dirty knives she was carrying clattered to the floor. She bent to pick them up. "That sounds fine," she said in a muffled voice.

There was no reason for her to be so immediately and furiously angry. He was only obeying the contract, the conditions she'd laid down from the start.

He added, "I'll probably go out for a hike first thing in the morning...that's my usual routine when I'm here."

And you're not invited: she didn't have to be a genius to figure that one out. Celia stuffed the knives into the dishwasher and grabbed the cloth, scrubbing at the pine table as though her life depended on it. When she was finished, she carried her case upstairs to the loft.

Jethro's bedroom. More books, a vivid quilt in primary colors on the king-sized bed and another luxurious bathroom. She unpacked, hanging a few things in his wardrobe, in which, elusively, she caught the scent of his body. Then she changed into jeans and a loose jade-green sweater, pulling the pins from her hair and tying it back in a pony tail.

She felt both overstimulated and exhausted; but how could she go to bed when Jethro was sitting so peacefully by the fireplace, his nose buried in a book? If this were the Caribbean, she could have gone for a swim; or if it were Paris, to the theater. She took her jacket from the wardrobe and went downstairs. "I'm going out to see the stars," she said.

He glanced up, giving her a preoccupied smile. "Sure…if you follow the stream, you can't get lost."

She went outside, shutting the front door with a decisive snap. The air was cool and fragrant, the stars shining as brightly here as they did in Collings Cove, and she'd never felt so lonely in her life. She tramped over the grass to the stream, her hands shoved in her pockets, sat down on a rock and gazed into the water.

It gave her no answers and did nothing to soothe the tumult of emotion in her breast. She'd got what she wanted. No sex. None of the kisses that sent her pulses skyrocketing, or the caresses that awakened in her the compelling ache of desire. Jethro was leaving her strictly alone; behaving as differently from Darryl as was possible. She should be down on her knees in gratitude, she thought, poking at the moss with a stick. Instead of which she felt frustrated, vulnerable and enraged. All at the same time.

It made no sense.

Half an hour later, Celia went back indoors. Jethro was putting another log on the fire; he'd changed into jeans and a cotton shirt, the fabric pulled taut across his back as he tossed the chunk of wood onto the flames. He was in his sock feet, his hair ruffled, a glass of red wine on the table by his chair. She said with artificial brightness, "I think I'll go to bed, it's been a busy day."

"Want anything before you go?"

And if that didn't top the list of unanswerable questions, nothing could. "No, thanks. See you in the morning."

He'd already gone back to his book and grunted something indecipherable. If she'd been lonely outdoors, Celia was now so angry she could barely see. In the upstairs bathroom she yanked on her satin nightgown—chosen with a real honeymoon in mind?—turned off the lights and fell into bed. The bed where Jethro slept when he was here by himself.

Burrowing her head under the covers, she started counting sheep. Woolly ones, shorn ones, fat ones and thin ones; and sometime after midnight she fell into a deep sleep.

CHAPTER TEN

WHEN Celia woke, sunlight was falling across the bed through the skylights, and she knew intuitively that she had the lodge to herself. She padded downstairs. Jethro had left a note on the kitchen table. "Back sometime this afternoon—I've taken the mountain trail. Have a good day," it said.

She crumpled it up, threw it in the garbage and went to have a shower. She made sure that by midafternoon she was hiking in the opposite direction to him; when she got back, they ate dinner and read by the fireplace, although Celia afterward couldn't have repeated a word of what was on the page. She was in bed by nine-thirty and tossed and turned most of the night.

Monday was much like Sunday, except her tension level had jumped another notch and Jethro was even more assiduously avoiding her. They'd be heading back to Washington early tomorrow morning, Celia thought, standing at the living-room window and watching Jethro chop wood. The honeymoon would be over.

It had been over before it began.

He'd taken off his shirt and the play of muscles in his torso as he swung the ax filled her with an agony of desire. She forced it away. She'd walk up the mountain trail today; Jethro had told her he'd built a small cabin up there. It would give her an excuse to be gone most of the day.

She couldn't wait to see the last of this place.

He was working with a concentrated ferocity, the logs splitting cleanly, the thunk of the ax echoing against the hillside. Every now and then he stopped to fling the slabs of wood in a pile to one side. Tearing her eyes away, she went to get a cup of coffee, adding twice her normal allotment of sugar and cream. Then the door burst open and Jethro came in, one hand wrapped around the other. With a pang of terror she saw bright drops of blood spattering the pine floor. "Jethro…"

"It's nothing," he rasped, "a splinter, that's all," and pushed past her.

She followed him into the downstairs bathroom, where he'd already turned on the cold tap. She said with a calmness she was far from feeling, "That's not a splinter, it's a chunk of kindling."

The wood chip was jammed into the soft flesh at the base of his thumb. He said tightly, "Have you got any tweezers?"

She was back in less than a minute. He'd doused his hand with disinfectant; she poured some over the tweezers and said, "Hold still."

"I can do it, Celia!"

"You can't! Stop arguing," she flared, and grabbed his hand in hers. But as she bent her head, tugging at the end of the splinter, her touch was very gentle. She heard his sharp indrawn breath as she worked the fragment of wood free. "Sorry," she muttered, "I know this must hurt."

A small sliver was left. Biting her lip, she got it in the tip of the tweezers and edged it from his flesh. Then she dabbed more disinfectant on the wound, feeling his flinch in every nerve of her body. "Phew," she said raggedly, "I'm glad that's over. Where do you keep the Band-Aids?"

"Cupboard over the sink."

She taped a couple of them over his torn skin. "That should stop the bleeding," she said and glanced up at him.

His big body was entirely too close. Dark hair curled on his chest; she could have reached out and touched the corded muscles of his belly, while his steel-blue eyes seemed to drill their way into her soul. He looked homicidal, she thought with an inward shudder, and backed away from him. "I—I'm going for a walk. If you're okay. Up the mountain."

"Go right ahead," he rasped.

"Do you have to make it so obvious you can't stand the sight of me?"

"You're the one who started this, who said no sex."

The tang of male sweat tantalized her nostrils; the shadows under his collarbones made her weak at the knees. What if she touched him, running her finger from breastbone to navel? Or reached up and pressed her mouth to his? Would he push her away? Or would he take her in his arms and kiss her as she longed to be kissed?

Don't, Celia.

Stepping backward, she nearly tripped over the bathmat, blushing with shame that she was so transparent to him, so easily read. "I—I expect I'll be gone most of the day."

"Keep an eye on the weather."

"You sound just like my father!"

"You didn't marry your father," Jethro snarled. "You married me—you might want to remember that."

How could she forget when every waking moment during this farce of a honeymoon she'd been so acutely aware of Jethro? Right now all she wanted to do was haul him off to the nearest bed and lose herself in him, become part of him as she'd never been part of a man...oh God, Celia thought, get me out of here. Whirling, she ran from the room.

Grabbing her haversack on the way, she hurried out of

looked or felt worse. And she was in no mood to be conciliatory. "We're not all perfect like you," she retorted. "Am I still the most beautiful woman you've ever seen?"

"Are you still planning to divorce me when it suits you?"

"I'll divorce you when my father's gone...." The words replayed themselves in her head, and in sudden despair she cried, "I can't stand this, I just can't bear it—I'm sorry, I should never have opened my mouth. Jethro, I'm cold, I've got to have a shower."

She bent to unlace her sodden boots. But her fingers wouldn't work and with an impatient exclamation Jethro knelt to undo them for her. The light fell on his thick, dark curls and his broad shoulders; she felt as though her heart was breaking. Then he stood up, his eyes boring into hers, and for moment filled with a wild, incredulous joy she thought he was going to take her in his arms. But then he stepped back, his shoulders a rigid line, and said with ice-cold exactitude, "I'll get supper while you're in the shower. It's past time for this ridiculous honeymoon to be over."

Once the honeymoon's over, you can go back to your woman in New York.

She'd thought the words. Not said them. Celia stumbled past him and went upstairs to get dry clothes.

An extensive low pressure system with more thunderstorms delayed their flights the next day; so it was nearly midnight when Celia and Jethro arrived back at Fernleigh. Jethro went straight to the rooms where he'd been staying before the wedding; Celia, dazed with tiredness, fell into her own bed and was asleep in minutes.

The next morning she dressed carefully in a becoming apple-green dress, leaving her hair loose as a distraction from her face, and applying makeup to hide the marks of exhaustion and unhappiness. Then she went in search of her father. He was in the breakfast room, reading the paper. "Ah, there you are, Celia," he said. "Jethro's beaten both of us to it—he's gone out for a run. How are you, dear?"

A simple enough endearment, yet it made her voice wobble. "Fine," she said.

He gave her a keen look. "Good honeymoon?"

If she disregarded the minor detail of no sex. Wishing those last two words had never been invented, Celia said airily, "Lovely. You look better, Dad...there's color in your cheeks and you look more rested."

Rustling the papers, Ellis said absently, "The doc's put me on some new drug."

"Dr. Kenniston? A new drug? What is it?"

"Oh, some polysyllabic name," Ellis said vaguely. "The specialists recommended it. What are your plans for the day?"

"Are the effects long-term?" she demanded.

"Don't fuss, Celia.... I wouldn't have told you if I'd thought you'd get your hopes up. By the way, I want you to go to the attic for me, there's a trunk of old photos of your mother up there. I've got the key here somewhere."

"A whole trunkful?" she said, distracted.

"Why don't you go through them? Bring some down with you, and I'll see what I can tell you about them."

"Oh Dad, I'd love that," she said, and took the small metal key from him.

"But have some breakfast first."

As she ate grapefruit and toast, she managed by a judicious blend of fact and fiction to paint a glowing portrait of the lodge and her honeymoon. Luckily, Jethro didn't come back to hear any of it. Then she kissed her father on the cheek. "I won't be long."

"Take your time."

She ran upstairs, down the hall and up the back stairs that wound their way to the attic. She'd always loved the attic as a child: it was a place of escape and fantasy, where the adults didn't bother her. Although carpeted and clean, it was full of shadows, the air warm with secrets.

It only took a few minutes to locate the trunk; the key turned sweetly in the lock and she opened the lid. Right on top lay a shawl of faded carmine silk; her fingers trembling, she lifted it out. It still smelled of perfume. Her mother's perfume, she thought with an ache in her throat, and remembered that evening so long ago when she'd seen her mother in her father's embrace, red silk round her mother's shoulders.

Biting her lip, Celia laid the shawl on the carpet. Then she took out some old yearbooks of her parents', searching until she found their pictures. And finally she picked up several bundles of photos and letters. Sitting back on the carmine shawl, she started going through them.

Fifteen minutes later, she was gazing at a drawing she'd done when she was four years old. Her mother had labelled it and on the back had written, "Celia's such a joy to me, so full of life and chatter and laughter. I love her dearly."

Helplessly, Celia began to weep, tears dripping down the front of her dress and onto the drawing. Then a floorboard creaked behind her and with a strange sense of presentiment she heard Jethro speak. "Celia...what's the matter? Don't cry, I hate to see you cry."

As he stooped beside her, she looked full at him. He couldn't be faking the concern in his face, he couldn't. She fell into his arms very naturally, because isn't that where she'd craved to be ever since she'd met him? Her tears soaking into the front of his shirt, she sobbed, "My m-mother really loved me, Jethro, it says so on that piece of paper. I wish she hadn't died so I could have gotten to know her better."

He settled himself more comfortably, pulling her into his lap and stroking her shoulders as she wept, pressing a handkerchief into her fingers as she gradually quietened. She blew her nose and scrubbed at her eyes, smiling at him unsteadily. "I must look a fright."

Jethro's answer was to pull her closer. His head plummeted to hers; he sealed her lips with his own in a kiss that Celia welcomed with all her heart and never wanted to end. She forgot about everything but Jethro: the taut bands of his arms around her body; the scent of his skin, so well known to her; the heat of his mouth on hers, the thrust of his tongue, his deep groan of pleasure as she opened to him, her own tongue playing with his.

Then he was easing her down onto the carpet, his body covering her, his mouth trailing the length of her throat to kiss the pulse at its base. Her body arched to meet him, her hands clutching his shoulders and pulling him closer, her every move revealing how much she wanted him. He kissed her again, a hungry kiss full of intensity, and muttered against her lips, "We should go downstairs. A bed would be more comfortable...."

She couldn't bear for the spell to be shattered. "No," she whispered, "I want to make love to you here, Jethro."

For a moment his head reared up, his eyes intent on her flushed face. "Say that again."

Her flush deepened. "I want to make love to you here," she repeated, and knew the words for the truth. There wasn't another woman in Jethro's life, there couldn't be. He wouldn't be so hungry for her, so intent on pleasing her if she weren't the only one.... She drew his face down, kissing the hard line of his jaw, the hollows under his cheekbones, before moving back to his mouth. Tracing his lower lip with her tongue, she murmured, "You taste good."

He gave an exultant laugh, letting the weight of his hips rest on her and thrusting with his body so that she felt all of his hardness. Desire was like a flower blossoming in her belly, like fire racing through her limbs; she thrust back, watching his face change, feeling him fumble with the buttons on her dress. Then he was lifting her so he could ease the dress over her head.

Suddenly shy, she saw him encompass the curves of her body in one burning glance. As he hauled his shirt off, throwing it to one side, she reached up and ran her fingers from the tautness of his throat down the hard muscles of his chest, tugging at his body hair, her face intent on its task. Her breasts moved gently in their lacy bra; with a muffled groan, Jethro dropped his head to her cleavage, nuzzling her ivory skin. She clasped him to her, her eyes shut, her whole being focused on the sheer sensuality of his exploration.

Her bra joined her dress and his shirt on the carpet. The expression on his face as he stroked her breast to its tip made her feel both her power as a woman and an incredible humility. Not knowing quite how to deal with this, she muttered, "Your belt's digging into me."

"Can't have that," he said huskily, and quickly stripped off the rest of his clothes. His body was beautiful to her, its smooth planes and strong, muscular curves; for a moment she gazed at him in pure delight. He said in a strange voice, "What's the matter, Celia? You've seen a naked man before."

Darryl. A shadow crossed her face. She didn't want to

think about Darryl, not now, not when she was in Jethro's arms. Jethro said edgily, "I'm sorry—I shouldn't have reminded you."

"You're not like Darryl," Celia said confidently, and twined her legs with his, kissing him with all the passion he unleashed in her simply by being there.

He was dropping a series of little kisses on her cheeks and her throat. "I want you to enjoy this, Celia."

She laughed, the dark brown of her irises illumined by tiny sparks. "Enjoy? I adore what you're doing to me!"

For a moment he looked up, smiling at her with none of the barriers behind which he so often hid himself. "You do, huh? But I've scarcely started."

"I also adore the way those little lines around your eyes crinkle up when you smile," she said rashly.

He laughed, his eyes very blue. "You're very good for my self-esteem," he said. Then, not hurrying, he moved down her body to her breasts, taking first one nipple, then the other in his mouth, tugging at her flesh with exquisite gentleness, until she wondered if she could die with pleasure. "Oh," she said in a voice of discovery. "Oh, Jethro, again, please."

Knowing she was venturing into new territory, territory far riskier, but also far more exciting, than her first solo flight, she stroked his face, learning through her fingertips the contours of his jaw and cheekbones, the softness of his hair. Then he took her hand in his and guided it lower, down his chest to his belly, then lower still. As she touched for the first time the silken hardness that was his essence, she was overwhelmed by a confusion of shyness and desire, a desire stronger than she could have imagined possible. She said faintly, "Jethro..."

He kissed her again, fiercely and possessively, as though claiming her for his own. She clasped him by the hips, learning the solidity of bone and the ripple of muscle, intoxicated by his closeness and her new freedom to explore it. With a breathless laugh she moved her hips against his, her awkwardness, had she but known it, a message in itself. But she was too absorbed in sensations utterly new to her to notice the brief perplexity in his eyes, his smallest of hesitations.

His body hair rasped her skin. She rubbed her cheek into the hollow under his collarbone, closing her eyes to savor the warmth of his skin, then moving her lips to his nipple; his gasp of pleasure filled her with pride and triumph.

As if her action had freed him from restraint, Jethro fell on top of her, spreading her hair like a glowing fan on the carmine shawl. They kissed and touched, hunger matching hunger, passion igniting still greater passion. Then Jethro found the crevice of her thighs, his fingers seeking out all her secret heat and wetness, until she was panting and writhing beneath him, moaning his name over and over again. Swiftly he slid into her.

There was an instant's resistance; a flash of pain crossed her face. He froze, poised over her. "Celia—"

Beyond caution or restraint, Celia begged, "Don't stop, Jethro, please."

His face was blank; he sounded oddly unsure of himself. "You told me you'd only once...but—"

Her answer was to lift her hips beneath him and thrust upward. And then the rhythms of her own body, so intimately joined to his, seized her. She cried out his name and from a long way away felt him within her, deeper and deeper, carrying her with him through the wildness of storm to the safest of havens.

To the place where she was inseparable from him and yet most truly herself.

CHAPTER ELEVEN

SLOWLY Celia came back to the present. To Jethro's sweat-slick forehead resting on her breast, to the hammering of her own heart and the heavy echo of his. She let one hand drift down his spine, tracing the small bumps of his vertebrae with infinite tenderness. "I didn't know it would be so…there aren't even any words. Except to say thank you."

He lifted his head. She'd never seen his face so naked to her, so exposed; her throat clogged with emotion. He said with none of his usual self-control, "You'd more or less told me you were a virgin. I didn't believe you—couldn't believe you. I should have. Because it was true."

"Yes, it was true." She rubbed her nose against his chin, wanting to relieve the strain on his features. "It's not true any more though."

He said evenly, "I don't know how to say this, Celia. I don't even know what I'm trying to say." He pushed himself up on his elbow, putting distance between them. "You trusted me enough to be the first one, didn't you? To undo the damage Darryl did."

Shouldn't she have? With a tiny clutch of dismay she felt cool air brush her skin where moments before there had only been the heat of Jethro's body welded to hers. She said uncertainly, "I guess so…" She had no idea what he was thinking. In a rush she added, "I must have been clumsy. Inexperienced. I'm sorry—"

"For God's sake," he said hoarsely, "that's not what I mean." He ran his fingers through his hair. Then his

138

eyes sharpened. "You're getting cold, you'd better get dressed. And I can't imagine you're comfortable on the floor."

She'd totally forgotten that she was flat on her back on the attic carpet. Her clothes were scattered around her; she grabbed for her lacy underwear and scrambled gracelessly to her feet, her hair falling forward to hide her face as she pulled them on. She didn't have a clue how Jethro felt right now; and she lacked the courage to ask.

Because she was scared of the answers?

Had she been wrong to trust him? Had he liked making love to her? Or had she bored him with her ineptitude? Finally, there was the most difficult question of all. How could it be over so soon, that magical, spontaneous joining of her flesh to his?

She heard the small sounds of him pulling on his trousers and doing up his zipper and didn't dare look at him. She'd learned something in the last half hour: that slalom skiing and piloting her own plane weren't the true risks. Emotional honesty was. It was a risk she clearly wasn't prepared to take.

Into Celia's anxiety fell one more strand, her earlier conviction that Jethro had another woman, a mistress in the city that was his home: the reason he hadn't touched his wife on his honeymoon.

He couldn't have another woman, she thought painfully, bending to get her dress. Surely he couldn't have made love a few moments ago with such single-minded passion if she, Celia, weren't the only one? As she struggled with the buttons, buttons Jethro had undone to bare her breasts, she was aware of him buckling his belt and picking up his shirt. She felt as though she had dropped from heaven to limbo from one second to the next. *Exile*, she thought. *So that's what that word really means. This horrible sense of loss. Of distance. This terror that what was between Jethro and me a few minutes ago is over, almost as if it had never happened.*

She wouldn't cry. Crying had gotten her into trouble in the first place, and she had too much pride to let Jethro see how bereft she was feeling. Act, Celia. Act.

Shoving her feet into her shoes before heading for the stairs, she said with just the right lightness, "My father will be wondering what I'm up to—I came to get some photos."

"He mentioned you were up here…that's how I found you. Why are you in such an all-fired hurry to leave?"

He was so tall, so overwhelmingly male. So intimately hers and so horribly distant from her. Agony rose like a tide in her body. "He's waiting," she said sharply. "Do you really want him to know what we were doing?"

"Are you ashamed of what we did?"

"Should I be?"

"Look, I shouldn't have—"

In pure panic, because she couldn't bear to hear him say he shouldn't have made love to her, Celia whirled and fled down the stairs. Her cheeks, she was sure, were bright red and anyone looking at her would know exactly how she'd spent the last half hour. She hurried along the hall, picturing icebergs and glaciers and blizzards, anything to cool her face. Did she look different? Would her father know why she'd been so long in the attic? As she took the second flight of stairs more moderately, she could hear Jethro hard on her heels. Over her shoulder she said with a valiant attempt to sound casual, "Why were you looking for me?"

Then Ellis came out of the breakfast room, leaning on his cane. "Ah, there you are," he said. "Did you have any luck?"

She'd left the photos in the attic on the floor. Along with her virginity. "Oh. Oh yes," she stammered, "I'm sorry it took so long."

"No matter...you'll be busy getting ready to go to New York, we can talk another day."

Jethro interjected, "I'm off to Manhattan after lunch, Celia—something's come up that I should deal with in person."

Manhattan. His other woman. The honeymoon's over, she thought sickly, all her suspicions flooding back full force. "Dad," she said, "I'm not going with Jethro. I'd rather be here with you."

Ellis said didactically, "A woman's first duty is to her husband."

"That kind of thinking went out with the bustle," she retorted.

"The two of you should make Manhattan your base," Ellis went on. "A bad idea to start a marriage with separate domiciles."

The phrase was worthy of the contract between her and Jethro. "But I want to be with you in the time we have left," she cried. Forcing the words past the lump in her throat, she added, "Jethro and I will have the rest of our lives together."

"You must go with him today, Celia. I insist. And I think you should look for a house there. A place that belongs to both of you."

There'd never been any use arguing when Ellis used that tone. She didn't want to go to New York. Jethro certainly didn't want her there. But she had to go. She said flatly, "I'll be back on Friday at the very latest."

"Good. While you were in Vermont, I had Melcher organize a party for a week from Saturday, the invitations went out on Monday. To celebrate your wedding. Caterers, florists, it's all arranged. Get a new dress while you're in Manhattan, Celia, do me proud.''

She wanted to yell and scream and stamp her feet. She did none of these things. ''That'll be fun,'' she said. ''Dancing?''

''A sedate chamber orchestra for us old folks, some wild-haired group with a very weird name for you youngsters.''

Her father actually seemed to be joking again. Her father was happy that she was married. Celia said, tossing her head, ''Next time, Dad, consult with me beforehand—considering it's my marriage we're celebrating. And now I guess I'd better go pack. What time are we leaving, Jethro?''

''As soon as you're ready.''

She hated not knowing what Jethro was thinking. Hated being pushed around the board like a chess piece. She turned in a swirl of skirts and ran upstairs; and in what seemed like no time, now wearing tailored trousers and a tangerine linen jacket with her hair in a smooth braid, Celia found herself following Jethro through the door into his Manhattan loft.

''I've got to hurry,'' he said in an abstracted voice. ''I hope this meeting won't take long. I should be back by seven, and we'll go for dinner. Here's an extra key if you go out.''

He'd spent the short flight with his nose buried in spread sheets, his mind obviously anywhere but on her. She took the key, for a moment staring at the fingers that had touched her so intimately such a short time ago. ''Good luck,'' she said with a cool smile.

His jaw tightened. ''I know I'm not—hell, this is no time to start anything. I'll see you later.''

The door clicked shut behind him. She snapped the lock and leaned back on the oak panels, closing her eyes, trying to breathe through the tightness in her chest. Did he really have a meeting? Or had it been a pretext and he was now frustrated and angry to be saddled with his wife in the city where he was normally a free agent?

She had no answers to questions she hated herself for asking. Slowly she opened her eyes and gazed around her. Space and light, polished wood floors and some startlingly beautiful modernistic sculptures, along with furniture of Finnish design whose clean lines delighted her. How could she love Jethro's personal spaces so much when the man himself was so distant from her?

She wandered around, admiring his collection of abstracts, the absence of clutter, skimming the bookshelves with their eclectic array of titles. He had a huge assortment of CDs along with top-of-the-line audio equipment. One whole shelf was nothing but operas. Operas? Jethro? All that emotion?

She gazed at the CDs. They didn't fit her picture of him. He'd made love to her with passion and with the intent to please her—or so it had seemed, even in her ignorance—and then he'd retreated as if it had never happened. Like a tap: turn it on, turn it off.

Her body had betrayed her. She was vulnerable to him now, for he'd shown her the lure and intensity of sexual consummation. But it was sex without emotion, without any deeper commitment than to the moment.

She wandered over to the tall windows which overlooked the Hudson River; a tug was hauling a barge under the bridge. Jethro had left her a phone number where he could be reached. So he must have a meeting. Was he phoning his mistress before he got there? Alerting her that his wife was with him?

Stop it, Celia, she scolded herself. Your imagination's working overtime and you've no evidence that Jethro has another woman. Go out for a run. Go shopping. Behave like a tourist. But don't stand here torturing yourself.

She'd packed her running gear and it was broad daylight; she'd head for Central Park. Then she'd go shopping. Anything to keep busy. Anything to keep her emotions at bay.

She ran for the better part of an hour, breathing in exhaust fumes, dodging pedestrians, deafened by the aggressive hornblasts of the taxis and trucks. Then she went back to the loft, showered, changed back into her trousers and jacket and strolled along Fifth Avenue. She found a very glamorous midnight-blue dress in shot taffeta that would be fine for her father's party; she bought a book about bush pilots and a ski magazine. By six-fifty she was back in the loft. No Jethro. No message on his voice mail.

She tried to read. She stared at the abstracts, wondering how he perceived them, what meanings they held for him and what their appeal was. But how could she possibly know? He'd never talked about himself, his friends, his parents, or the way he'd brought up his sister Lindy. His mother had abandoned Jethro when he was very young, leaving him to the mercies of a father who drank too much. Surely that had affected him, had had something to do with making him the man he was. Celia gave a heavy sigh. He was a mystery to her, this man whose body so entranced her.

Wandering nearer the tall windows, she stroked the cool metallic curves of the largest sculpture. It was now quarter to eight. He was forty-five minutes late. Pushing open the door of Jethro's bedroom, Celia walked in.

Doing her best to ignore the wide bed, she opened his closets, finding arrays of suits and casual wear, but nothing remotely feminine. Nor did the bathroom yield perfume or a woman's expensive soap or a negligee hanging on the back of the door.

I despise myself for doing this, Celia thought with utter clarity. I'm spying on my husband because I'm jealous. Because I can't bear to think of him with another woman. Where is he? Why hasn't he come home?

Jethro had gotten exactly what he'd wanted out of the meeting. He'd had to hang tough, using all his wits and experience during the negotiations. But he'd won. Only drawback was, he'd have to spend most of next week in Australia and Singapore.

As he got in his limousine, he pushed back his cuff. Five to eight. Goddammit, he thought, I told Celia I'd be back by seven. He pushed the glass panel open and said to his chauffeur, "I'm late, Henry. Hurry it up, will you?"

"Yes, sir. Traffic's heavy though."

No use to call Celia. She already knew he was late. He started flipping through the glossy real estate magazine he'd borrowed from his chief assistant, pausing every now and then at a property that might interest Celia. But the pictures didn't hold his attention; drumming on his knee with his fingertips, he wondered if he shouldn't have phoned her after all. But they were only two blocks from the loft. No point now.

Sure, Jethro. You can negotiate one of the most difficult deals of the last three years yet you can't make a simple decision about phoning your wife?

His wife. He still couldn't get used to those words. Had no clue what they really meant to him. He hadn't intended making love to Celia this morning. Not part of his plan. He'd meant to wait until she made the first move.

She hadn't liked the way he'd kept his distance at the

lodge. Not that it had been easy to do. Far from it. It had nearly driven him crazy living in such close quarters with her and not so much as laying a finger on her.

So why had he done it? To show her who was the boss? To prove to himself that his much-vaunted control was still very much in place, despite her presence? Or—a little more admirably—to allow her the choice, so he'd know she wasn't equating him with Darryl?

Whatever the reason, this morning all his resolve had shattered. The sight of her crouched, weeping, on the attic carpet had cut him to the heart.

The heart. So did he have one where Celia was concerned? Certainly his initial urge this morning had been the simple wish to comfort. Only afterward, when she'd raised her face and smiled at him, had his baser instincts taken over. *I want to make love to you*, she'd said. So they had.

She'd been a virgin. There'd been no other man. He was still recovering from that mind-bending revelation.

She'd trusted him with her body and her feelings. A gift worth more than any rare yellow diamond.

With a flourish Henry drew up at the sidewalk. "Here we are, sir."

"Thanks," Jethro muttered and jumped out. He found himself running up the stairs to the loft rather than waiting for the elevator. Opening his door with an impatience new to him, he called, "Celia?"

She came out of his bedroom, her face set. She was wearing a black dress startling in its simplicity, her hair a vivid aureole around her face; as always, her beauty struck him like a blow. "Sorry I'm so late," he said, dropping his briefcase on the table. "Won't take me long to change. You might want to flip through this magazine, there are a couple of penthouses we might look at."

She said in a voice like ice, "I have no intention of buying property in New York."

He flung his jacket on the nearest chair and yanked at his tie. "I'd be buying it," he said with more bluntness than tact.

"Not for me, you won't."

He started unbuttoning his shirt, frowning at her. "I apologized for being late, Celia."

"You're forgetting something. This is a fake marriage. A temporary marriage. There's no need for us to own a penthouse, no matter what my father says."

"You're spoiling for a fight, aren't you?"

"What's her name, Jethro?" Celia said very quietly.

His shirt was hanging open. His jaw was probably hanging open, too. "Whose name?"

"The woman—your mistress. The reason you didn't come near me on our honeymoon. The reason you're so late home."

He stepped closer. Her face was pale, her eyes enormous; she was so tense, he had the feeling she'd break into pieces if he touched her.

He wanted to touch her. He always did. Keeping his voice level with a huge effort, he asked, "Are you accusing me of being with another woman the last few hours?"

For once she didn't make a flip retort. "Yes," she said.

His chest was engulfed in a storm of anger and pain. The anger he understood. But pain? He never let a woman close enough to cause him pain. Each word dropping like a stone, he said, "I wasn't with a woman. I was at a meeting—I can give you the names of witnesses if you don't believe me.'' He gave her a nasty smile. ''My rivals, just so you know there's no collusion.''

She was staring at him with unnerving fixity. ''At the lodge I might as well have been your maiden aunt. Or someone who was a complete turn-off. But then in the attic you made love to me.'' Her voice quivered ever so slightly. ''Ever since, you've acted as though I'm a stranger. You've—''

''Do you believe me?'' he demanded. ''Celia, there is no other woman.''

For a long moment she regarded him in silence. Except it wasn't really silence: his heart was hammering so loudly she must be able to hear it. Hell, they could hear it two stories down. ''Yes,'' she said with painful slowness, ''I do believe you that there's no one else. But why have you ignored me ever since we made love, Jethro? Was I that inept? That much of a disappointment?''

He remembered the luscious curve of her hip, her ardent and touchingly inexperienced movements, the joyous glow to her skin. When he'd gone up to the attic to tell her about the meeting in New York, he'd planned on keeping his distance. On obeying that goddammed contract until she made the first move. But he'd lost control.

The famous Lathem control. Out the attic window because the woman who was his wife had been weeping over a bunch of old papers as though her heart would break. Go slow, Jethro, he thought, feeling his nails dig into his palms. Tell her the truth. Or at least part of it. She deserves it. ''You weren't inept. You were so beautiful you took my breath away,'' he said.

She wrapped her arms around her chest and said jaggedly, ''I don't know any of the moves, I can't play all the games everyone else seems to play. That's one more reason I don't do the society thing, why I'm more at home in Collings Cove than Pennsylvania Avenue. I can look sophisticated, sure, anyone can do that. But when it comes to sex, I'm in kindergarten. Be honest, Jethro—you made love to me because you had to win. You had to show me how silly and immature I was to draw up that contract.'' Her laugh was bitter. ''No sex. How naive can you get?''

''I signed the contract, too. So what does that make me?''

''You're the only one who can answer that,'' she said. She frowned, obviously thinking hard. ''I keep saying we made love. We didn't though, did we? We just had sex.''

''That's a man's line,'' Jethro grated. ''Not a woman's.''

''You said I was unpredictable.''

''I didn't know the half of it!''

''Sex,'' she repeated determinedly. ''Just sex.''

Infuriated, he had the feeling she hadn't heard a word he'd said, that she was working things out to her own satisfaction in a way that had nothing to do with him. He said curtly, ''Cut out the word *just*, will you?''

To his secret delight, she blushed a vivid pink. ''You—you mean you liked it?''

''For Pete's sake, Celia—of course I did.'' That wild and unexpected mating on the carpet had transfixed him with its intensity, its inevitability and its sheer beauty. Or would *terrified* be a more accurate word? Either way, it had been enough to make any man allergic to commitment run a mile. And he sure fit that category.

''Then why—'' she began.

He'd had enough of words. Jethro stepped closer, took Celia in his arms and kissed her with a hunger that was bone-deep. Just as if he'd never made love to her, he thought distantly.

Never had sex with her. *Had sex.* How could those two

short words possibly encompass how overwhelming their union had been?

With a jolt to his gut, another possibility occurred to him. "Didn't you like it?"

She stared absorbedly at the buttons on his shirt. "I loved it.... Couldn't you tell?"

If she was in kindergarten, he was in playschool, he thought caustically. He'd always kept his sex life in control. He liked the women he bedded, but he never went beyond liking. Had never wanted to. Emotions were as remote from his bed as commitment.

With the disconcerting sense that nothing he'd accomplished in the boardroom over the past few hours had been remotely as important as this one small question, Jethro said, "Enough that you'd like to do it again?"

He felt the tremble run through her body. "Now, you mean?"

"I'd much prefer taking off that very sexy black dress to sitting across from it in a restaurant."

"Oh," said Celia. "Really?"

Some of the tension eased from his shoulders. "Really," he said.

"Could we do it in a bed this time?"

"Good idea." He glanced downward. "Oak floors aren't designed with sex in mind."

"Sex," she repeated. "That's all this is, Jethro."

"Of course. I wouldn't want it otherwise."

How the devil could one chestnut-haired woman make him feel so off balance, so riled up? He was getting precisely what he always wanted, sex without involvement; yet he felt like a kid whose favorite toy had just smashed into a thousand pieces. "We should use some protection this time," he said in a clipped voice.

Her eyes widened as she remembered how she and Jethro had gotten carried away in the attic. "I forgot all about that—I told you I was in kindergarten."

He was a great deal more experienced than she, and he hadn't thought of it, either; the sight of her weeping onto a red silk shawl had driven caution and common sense from his mind. Yet another of his ironclad rules gone by the board, he thought; how the hell could he have been so criminally careless? "I'll look after it," he said, and because there was no way he wanted her guessing his emotions were in such an uproar, he sounded as cold as an iced martini. "I need to have a shower, then let's go to bed. Afterward, we could order in Thai food."

That should put her in her place. Sex sandwiched between a shower and curried prawns.

Her chin tilted defiantly. "Don't take too long in the shower."

If only her courage and stubbornness, her sense of humor and her pure cussedness weren't such a challenge. He'd been looking for a new challenge. Well, he'd found one. And he hadn't had to fly to the Andes to do it. Shrugging out of his shirt, Jethro headed for the shower. He could have asked her to join him. He didn't. Enough was enough.

When Jethro walked back into his bedroom, a towel wrapped around his hips, Celia was tucked under the covers of his big bed, reading. As though there was nothing surprising about this, as though his bed were her territory. She was his wife, after all. If anyone belonged in his bed, she did.

Her nightgown, what he could see of it, looked minimal. God, how he wanted her! But did she need to know that?

She only had to look at him to realize it, he thought wryly, aware of the instant hardening of his groin. He walked over to the bed and sat down beside her. "What are you reading?"

"It's about bush pilots," she said, her eyes skidding from his bare chest back to the book. "Maybe that's what I'll do next. After..." her voice wavered momentarily. "Dad would hate me doing it, he'd think it was too dangerous."

"After we're divorced, you mean," Jethro said tersely. Bush pilots worked up north. A long way from Manhattan. About as far as you could get.

"How did this get to be so complicated?" she cried.

"Because our divorce hinges on your father's death and you love your father—that's how. One reason, anyway."

She was staring at the Twin Otter on the book's cover as though she'd never seen an aircraft before. "It's the only reason," she said stonily.

Nothing to do with him, in other words. "We're in an intolerable situation because of your father, don't think I'm not aware of that," he said tautly. "Both of us should have indulged in some hard thinking before we embarked on this absurd contract. Myself as much as you."

"You regret marrying me."

And how was he supposed to answer that? When the valley between her breasts was a deep shadow he longed to plunder, when her shoulders were silken curves and her parted lips a blatant invitation? His control was slipping again, he thought grimly. Along with the towel. "We are married, regret it or not," he said. "Put the book down, Celia."

Before she could argue, he leaned forward and kissed her hard, his tongue thrusting to taste all the sweetness of her mouth, his hand seeking out the warm swell of her breast, where the nipple hardened instantly to his touch. Her book slid to the floor with a small thud. She put her arms around his neck and kissed him back with a fervor that inflamed all his senses; this time she knew what to expect, he realized dimly, and was welcoming him with all the impetuous passion and generosity of her nature.

Celia. His wife. In his bed.

But it was only sex. They both knew that.

CHAPTER TWELVE

CELIA gave herself one last glance in the mirror. She was wearing the midnight-blue taffeta gown she'd found on Fifth Avenue; she looked, even to her own eyes, quite startlingly sophisticated. She also looked like a woman in a way she never had before.

The party to celebrate her marriage to Jethro was about to begin. Her marriage. The blusher on her cheeks became quite unnecessary as she remembered the two days last week that she'd spent in Manhattan with Jethro. Mostly in bed.

His body delighted her; in his wide bed they'd come together in lust, playfulness, laughter and tenderness. Twice she'd wept, overwhelmed by an intimacy beyond her experience or wildest fantasies.

And what about last night, when he'd come home from Singapore? He'd scarcely entered the door of their suite before he'd started shucking off his clothes. He'd picked her up and carried her to bed, fiercely impatient, as ardent and generous a lover as she could possibly have desired.

If he'd been ardent, she'd more than matched him.

She scowled at herself in the mirror. Their partnership was about sex. Earth-shattering sex, for sure. But still just sex. To make love you had to be in love. Or else the words were meaningless.

As meaningless as her marriage.

She was on a carousel, she thought unhappily, going round and round and never getting anywhere. Then she jumped like a startled kitten as a tap came on her door. "Come in," she called.

Ellis walked in. "Fix my tie, Celia," he said. "Your mother always did it for me—she looked lovely in blue, too."

Yesterday morning, she and Ellis had talked about Marian for the better part of two hours, each minute as precious to Celia as a jewel. And now she was struck again with how well her father looked; even better than he had earlier in the week. "You look great, Dad.... I can't get over it."

"Feeling a lot better," he said bluffly. "You never know, I might have this licked. The new medication's done wonders."

She hugged him hard, her voice breaking. "Oh, I do hope so.... It would make me so happy! I feel like we're just starting to get to know each other—I can't bear to lose you."

"Your marriage, too—that's got something to do with it. I couldn't have wished for a better husband for you than Jethro."

The turmoil of emotions this sentiment roused was becoming all too familiar to Celia. Of course she wanted her father on his way to recovery. With all her heart she prayed for it. Yet the inevitable corollary was that her marriage would be extended. Indefinitely. For how could she upset Ellis with a divorce only months after the marriage? She couldn't. She couldn't possibly jeopardize his health and well-being for her own selfish ends.

Jethro didn't want to be married to her indefinitely. He loved going to bed with her, she'd stake her life on that. But he didn't love her. His emotions were untouched by her; his control rigidly in place.

That silly phrase *no sex* had become obsolete upstairs

in the attic; and most certainly in the loft in Manhattan and last night in her bed. But another phrase was very much in place. *No love.* If Ellis recovered, Jethro would be stuck with a loveless marriage he hadn't bargained for and couldn't possibly want.

The same was true for her, of course.

What was the word Jethro had used? *Intolerable.*

"There," she said, "your tie's perfect. And I'm glad you're happy for me, Dad. I'll be down in a minute, I haven't decided on my jewelry yet."

"Save a dance for me," Ellis said, and planted a kiss on her forehead. "Not to the racket those electric guitars are making, though."

"It's old-fashioned rock and roll, Dad," she chuckled, and watched him leave the room. He looked almost sprightly, and how could she be at one and the same time so extraordinarily happy and so utterly miserable?

She was rummaging in her jewel case, trying to decide if she preferred gold rather than silver with her dress, when Jethro opened her door; they were sharing her suite of rooms. He looked impossibly handsome in his tuxedo; her heart lurched in her breast. With as much poise as she could muster, she said, "You're the sexiest man I've ever gone to bed with, Jethro Lathem."

"Keep it that way," he said, his jaw a hard line, his eyes seeming to burn through her sleek gown to the body beneath. Her skin tingled; unconsciously she swayed toward him. "We haven't got time, Celia," he added, and pulled a flat box out of the pocket of his tux. "This is for you. A belated wedding present."

Her poise abandoned her; all the complicated feelings which Jethro roused simply by existing rushed back to torment her. "Please don't, Jethro! You and I both know this marriage is a sham. Let's at least be honest with each other.''

"You can't wait to be rid of me, can you?'' he said in an ugly voice.

"The same's true for you. Admit it.''

"Your father's getting better.''

Her brown eyes flared mutinously. "Then we'll just have to wait until he's strong enough to handle our divorce. Won't we?''

"Remind me next time someone shoves a contract under my nose to read the fine print,'' Jethro snarled. "In the meantime, your father, I'm sure, expects me to give you a wedding gift. So take it, will you?''

He'd only chosen the gift to please her father. Reluctantly Celia took the box, opening the lid. Against the white satin lining lay a wisp of gold chain set with two diamonds and a sapphire. It was very beautiful. "I don't understand how you can choose exactly what I like when you hate me for what I've done to you,'' she said unsteadily.

"So you like it?''

There was a note in his voice that made her look up. "It's exquisite, Jethro…thank you.''

As though the words were torn from him, he said, "It reminded me of you—delicacy, strength and beauty.''

"You sure know how to get to me,'' she mumbled.

"We've got that much in common.'' He lifted the chain from the box. "Hold still.''

Obediently she bent her head. His fingers brushed her nape, his breath wafting across her cheek; despite—or perhaps because of—their impassioned mating last night, she'd willingly have made love with him right now and too bad about all the guests who were waiting for them to appear. "There,'' Jethro said, "that's got it.''

He stepped back. The chain was so light it seemed to drift across her skin; the stones sparkled and glimmered. It was only a gift, she thought frantically. A gift of expedience. No reason to cry and every reason not to. "We'd better go...Dad will be wondering where we are."

Jethro put an arm around her waist, his smile ferocious. "We're madly in love, remember? All the society columnists are down there along with a good mix of your friends and mine—so act your head off, my darling wife."

The words came from nowhere, laced with desperation. "Sex—the way we are in bed—that's not an act, is it, Jethro?"

"If you don't know the answer to that, I'm sure as hell not going to tell you."

He was pushing her toward the door. She'd hurt him. She knew she had. "I'm sorry," she faltered, "I didn't mean—"

"Let's get this over with."

He looked anything but an adoring husband. She said coldly, "Both of us have got to act, Jethro," and swept out of the room ahead of him.

The ballrooms were at the back of the house on the ground floor; a circular staircase led to the reception area, which was decorated with tall standards of lilies. French crystal chandeliers sparkled and shone; the tall windows, hung with royal blue silk, overlooked a floodlit marble fountain in the boxwood garden.

At the top of the stairs, Jethro tucked her arm in his, smiled down at her with what she would have sworn was genuine tenderness, and murmured, "Madly in love... let's take them by storm, darling Celia."

His hand lay warm over hers; he was caressing her fingers, and his eyes wandered her face with possessive intimacy. *It's an act*, she thought breathlessly. *Only an act.*

I love him.

Rocked to her foundations, Celia clutched Jethro's sleeve. *I've fallen in love with my husband*, she thought, and knew the words for the simple truth. *I'm in love. In love with Jethro.* Her eyes widened with wonderment, joy blossoming in her heart as she gave him a brilliant, incautious smile.

The orchestra struck up the wedding march. The gathering of stylishly attired guests at the bottom of the stairs applauded and Celia's smile widened to include them. She began the descent, her hips swaying gracefully in her elegant gown.

In a savage whisper, Jethro said, "You'd be wasted as a bush pilot—Broadway's crying out for your talents."

His words sliced through a joy as fragile as it was new. He thought she was acting; he didn't recognize real emotion when it was right in front of his nose. A real emotion he certainly didn't share. *Later*, Celia thought feverishly. *Later I'll worry about what this all means. But for now I have to behave like Jethro's loving wife.*

I don't have to act.

Her father was waiting at the base of the stairs. She kissed him and said, "You get the second dance, Dad. The first one belongs to Jethro...doesn't it, darling?"

His fingers tightened cruelly on hers. But no one could have faulted the way he was looking at her, with a mixture of passion and adoration that made her tremble to the roots of her being. He led her out on the dance floor, pulling her against his hips, his cheek resting on her hair. Desire flooded her; she surrendered to it in a way new to her, for it was a desire impelled by love.

She wanted this dance to last forever.

It didn't, of course. A few minutes later Celia had to relinquish Jethro's arm to take her father's. She danced with Ellis, her brother and Lindy's husband; with Jethro again, with her lawyer, her father's accountant, and then with Dave. She liked Dave. There was something about his steady gray eyes that inspired trust. He said, leading her expertly through a foxtrot, "Jethro looks head over heels in love for a guy I figured was immune to commitment."

Celia blurted, "What was his father like, Dave?"

"The less said about him the better."

"That's certainly the way Jethro handles it," she replied, an edge to her voice.

Briefly Dave lost the rhythm. "Clyde Lathem was a boor when he was sober and as dangerous as a roomful of explosives in a burning house when he wasn't. Jethro took on the responsibility for Lindy when he was far too young, and he had to stand up against a man who wasn't above using his fists when all else failed."

It was Celia's turn to miss a step. "So where do you fit in the picture?"

"Oh, I helped him out here and there."

"How?"

"Persistent, aren't you?"

"I'm married to Jethro, Dave," she said drily.

"Then I think you should ask Jethro."

"Is that what you call male solidarity?"

"You've got a lifetime ahead of you, Celia," Dave said mildly.

Not with Jethro, she didn't. As the foxtrot ended, Dave added, "Jethro might not be the easiest man to live with, but he's true to the core. Now, how about we find something to eat?"

So Celia ate and drank, accepting congratulations as her

due, the wishes for happiness as an already accomplished fact. The noise level increased; the party was a success. Time to repair her lipstick, she thought, and left the main ballroom with its baroque ceiling and expanse of gleaming floor for the nearest washroom. As she walked behind a gorgeous array of tropical plants, she came face-to-face with Darryl Coates.

Her father must have invited him despite Darryl's messy divorce; Darryl's father and Ellis were old business partners. Darryl had been drinking, his cheeks were mottled and his tie askew. "Saw you coming this way and thought I'd wait for you...clever little Celia," he sneered. "You've done very well for yourself—no wonder you weren't interested in me."

"You know why I'm not interested in you."

"Come off it." Darryl made a rough grab for her; as she pulled back, he lurched on his feet, his kiss missing her mouth and smearing her cheek.

"Don't!" she choked.

In a voice like ice, Jethro said, "Leave my wife alone."

Darryl swayed sideways, pushing against the wall for support. "She only wanted a little kiss for old times' sake. Money's what she's after...expensive tastes, Celia has. Too expensive for the likes of me."

"I love Jethro for himself," Celia said clearly, "not for his money," and thought what a huge relief it was to speak the truth for once.

His fists clenched at his sides, Jethro said in a voice Celia hadn't heard before, "Coates, I never want to see you near Celia again. Because if I do, I won't be responsible for the consequences...do you understand?"

Darryl backed away. "Hey, man, you're overreacting. After all, it's not as if she's any great lay—"

In a blur of movement Jethro picked Darryl up and

thrust him hard against the wall. "One more word and it'll be the end of you," he snarled. "I know what you did to Celia four years ago. One phone call and you'd be finished in this town."

Then, as if the contact had sullied him, Jethro let go of Darryl, wiped his hands on his jacket and turned to Celia. "I came looking for you because your father wants to make a speech. He's waiting for us."

His arm around her waist felt like a steel bar. As Darryl staggered off toward the men's room, she said urgently, "Jethro, I didn't instigate that kiss."

"I never thought you did. Not your style."

"You mean you believe me?"

"For God's sake, Celia—you promised you wouldn't have an affair for the duration of this marriage and there's not an underhanded bone in your body. Of course I believe you."

"I don't think I'll understand you if I live to be a hundred!"

"Non-issue—we'll be divorced long before that," Jethro snapped, tugging at her arm. "Come on, your father's waiting by the podium."

"Don't be in such a hurry! This is important. You trust me—that's what you're saying."

Jethro stopped dead in his tracks. "Yeah, that's what I'm saying. So what?"

"That's the best compliment you could possibly have paid me."

"This marriage is about acting," he said with brutal exactitude. "Not about reality."

His words were like a slap in the face. For you it's about acting, she thought, a cold fist squeezing her heart. But not for me. She could never tell Jethro she was in love with him. He'd laugh all the way to the divorce court.

"You don't know how glad I'll be when this party's over," she said.

"No more than me. Let's go."

They'd reached the end of the row of hibiscus and canna lilies. She pasted a smile to her lips and made her way across the dance floor toward her father. His speech was mercifully brief, though undoubtedly sincere; Jethro, in his reply, sounded equally sincere. He sounded like a man who was deeply in love.

He should be on Broadway too, Celia thought miserably. The joy she'd felt at the top of the stairs had entirely dissipated; all she felt now was a vast emptiness. Pain, she knew, would come later. She couldn't afford to feel it now.

Her father was looking pale and drawn. When the orchestra had started up again and Jethro was dancing with Lindy on the far side of the floor, she took Ellis aside. "Dad, I think you should call it quits, you look really tired."

"My sentiments exactly."

The man who had spoken was a stranger to her. Ellis said, with an awkwardness rare to him, "I don't believe you two have met. Dr. Michael Stansey...my daughter, Celia. Michael's the one who put me on the new drug, Celia—he's the research scientist who came up with it in the first place."

The doctor shook her hand. "I'm delighted with your father's progress. As I'm sure you are, Mrs. Lathem." He gave her a boyish grin. "I must say, I never figured Jethro for anything but a confirmed bachelor."

"You know Jethro?" she said, puzzled.

The doctor looked surprised. "We've been colleagues for several years—he owns the pharmaceutical company that's been testing this new drug for the market. He's the one who phoned me to come and see your father…I thought you knew that.''

''He must have forgotten to mention it,'' Ellis said heartily. ''Early indications suggest my recovery will be complete, Celia. Good news, eh?''

''Marvellous news,'' she said, her brain whirling. ''And we have you to thank, Dr. Stansey.''

''The way your father's responded is all the thanks I need—far beyond my expectations. Well, I must find my wife, I have a conference in California tomorrow so we'll have to be leaving. All the best, Ellis, and I'll see you in a week for another check-up. Congratulations, Mrs. Lathem, Jethro's a fine man.''

As he moved out of earshot, Ellis said with a touch of bravado, ''Jethro asked me to keep the connection quiet. At least until after the wedding.''

''I see,'' she said noncommittally, and walked with her father to his wing of the house. At his door she asked as casually as she could, ''So Jethro set this up before the wedding?''

''That's right. The Tuesday before.''

The day Jethro had engineered her lunch with Lindy. ''That's why you kept to your room so much that week.''

''The drug made me dizzy and nauseated at first. And Jethro didn't want to get your hopes up for nothing…hence the secrecy.''

''Of course,'' she said. Then she added with true warmth, ''I'm just so glad it's working, Dad. And thanks for the lovely party, it was sweet of you to make all the arrangments.''

''You're a good daughter, Celia,'' Ellis mumbled, and yawned widely. ''I may not see you in the morning. Jethro mentioned he has to go to Atlanta, even though it's the weekend—I know you'll want to go with him.''

"Of course," she said again. "Good night, Dad."

The door closed behind him. Her heels tapping on the marble flooring, Celia went back to the party. The fight with Jethro could wait. It would keep, she thought bitterly.

Jethro might trust her. It was horribly obvious she shouldn't have trusted him.

Celia's last dance was with Jethro. Fueled by rage, she gyrated and swayed, her body a blatant invitation, her eyes glittering like the diamonds round her throat. As the final chord throbbed through the air, Jethro muttered for her ears alone, "Time to take you to bed, wife."

We'll see about that, she thought. They made their farewells to the last of the guests and went upstairs. As Jethro pulled the door shut, she leaned against it, her fists bunched behind her back. "I met Dr. Stansey this evening."

Jethro's mouth thinned. "Your father invited him—I didn't."

"Why wouldn't he invite the man who's saved his life?"

"I'd asked him not to."

"I'm sure you did." Her nostrils flared. "You've really made a fool of me from the beginning, haven't you, Jethro? First you let me offer you sixty thousand dollars. And then you marry me knowing there won't be a divorce in three months because of this wonder drug."

His eyes were watchful on her face. "The drug looked very promising—but Stansey couldn't give any guarantees. I didn't want to get your hopes up for nothing."

Just what her father had said. "I feel so...so humiliated, so stupid," she said in a low voice. "This is about *my* father. Not yours. Why didn't *I* find out about this drug myself? I trusted the specialists, that's why, the ones Dad had called in.''

"They're good men, Celia. Just not the best. Not the ones on the cutting edge.''

"I should have gotten more opinions!''

Jethro tugged at his tie. "If it hadn't been for the pharmaceutical connection, I wouldn't have known about the drug myself—stop beating up on yourself.''

"All right,'' she said with deadly precision, "I will. How about I beat up on you instead? If you'd told me about Dr. Stansey and the new drug, we wouldn't have had to get married. If I didn't know better, I'd think you *wanted* to marry me.''

Her voice had risen. Jethro exploded, "Why don't you try looking at it my way, Celia? There were no guarantees for the drug. It's worked—but it might not have.''

"Why did you marry me, Jethro?''

Ignoring her, he said furiously, "Would you rather I hadn't called Mike Stansey? Left your father to die? You think I could have lived with myself if I'd done that— just to save your precious feelings?''

"At least I've got feelings!''

"So have I,'' he snarled, raking his fingers through his hair. "I couldn't have looked myself in the mirror if I hadn't made every effort to save your father's life. Anyway, by then the marriage was set in motion, Ellis wouldn't have understood if you'd suddenly cried off.''

Her shoulders slumped. "You have an answer for everything, don't you? But don't you *see*? We're trapped, Jethro. Trapped in an empty marriage, deceiving the families we love—my father, your sister. I hate it, I just hate it!''

"You hate me—that's what you mean.''

Her voice shook. "I feel like I'm being torn apart.

You've saved my father's life, don't think I don't see that. So on the one hand I'm so grateful—''

''We're even,'' he said flatly. ''You saved my life, I saved your father's.''

She blurted, ''Did you love your father, Jethro?''

His face closed. ''That's irrelevant.''

''Is it? You never talk about your childhood—about your mother, or what it was like growing up with a man who used his fists on you and drank himself into an early grave. You even had to protect your sister from him.''

''Lindy talks too much,'' Jethro said curtly.

''Maybe you don't talk enough.'' Celia's brow furrowed. ''Maybe that's one thing marriages are for, a safe place where two people can be real and talk about the stuff that really matters... Because they trust each other. You said you trusted me, Jethro.''

''It's all in the past, there's no point talking about it!''

''Yes, there is,'' she persisted, her heart beating like a trip-hammer. ''That's what I've learned the last few days with my father, that the past can be redeemed.''

''For you, maybe.''

''But, Jethro—''

''Leave it, Celia! How do you redeem a man who within ten feet of a bottle of gin turned into a foul-mouthed brute? He dragged the Lathem name into the gutter and the family business along with it. And yeah, you're right—I never left Lindy alone with him.''

''How old were you when you started looking after her?''

''Nine, ten—I don't remember. He died when I was nineteen. You know why Dave's still my best friend? Because he was the only one who'd loan me money to get the business back on its feet. Everyone else laughed in my face." He jammed his fists into his pockets. "Just leave it, will you? It's nothing to do with you."

Her nails were digging into her palms. She meant nothing to him, that's what Jethro was really saying. She was someone he'd made a temporary alliance with, not someone with whom he'd share his feelings. As exhaustion overwhelmed her, Celia whispered, "I'm so grateful to you for my father's sake, and yet I loathe what you've done to me. Deceived me, humiliated me, used me for ends I can't begin to fathom. You don't want to be married to me, I know you don't."

Jethro threw his jacket on the nearest chair and walked over to her, running his palm from her bare shoulder over the firm rise of her breast under the midnight-blue fabric. "There are benefits, Celia—or are you forgetting them?"

She shrank back against the door. "For you, marriage is only about sex."

"Only?"

She said with real anguish, "You're not bored in bed with me, are you, Jethro? So you've achieved your aim in marrying me."

His gaze was fastened on her face. "You love what we do in bed together, admit it."

He was still stroking her breast, slowly and hypnotically; she felt the deep ache of desire blossom in her belly. Useless to fight it. The power of his body over hers, and her own body's instinctive response to him were unconquerable. Yet how could she go to bed with him, knowing he was only assuaging boredom? Now that she loved him, such knowledge was unbearable.

But she couldn't leave him. Not yet. Ellis's health was still too fragile for that. Maybe, just maybe, in a month or two she could tell her father the true story of her marriage. Explain the whole sorry mess, and trust he'd understand that she'd acted for the best. With his interests at heart.

In the meantime, she had to hide her feelings from Jethro. How he'd laugh if he knew she'd fallen in love with him! One more woman lying at his feet for him to trample.

But hiding her feelings meant more acting, she realized in despair.

Jethro slid his hands round her waist, smoothing the curves of her hips. As the hard wall of his chest rubbed against her breasts, her pulse quickened and the color rose in her cheeks. She said fiercely, "If you think you can make me beg you to stop, you're quite wrong."

His steel-blue eyes clashed with her brown ones. "That's one of the reasons I'm not bored with you, my darling Celia—you'll never beg me for anything, will you? Not if it kills you."

"You've got brains, Jethro, I'll give you that—you're not just a great body," she said, and saw anger flicker across his face.

Like a hawk to its prey, his head dropped to kiss her. It was a searing kiss, compounded of rage and desire, to which she more than responded. With all her newfound knowledge, she rubbed her hips into his erection, her blood racing through her veins. He found the zipper on the back of her dress and hauled on it; as the taffeta slithered down her body, she tugged at his shirt, burying her fingers in his body hair, the heat of his skin tripping her into needs only he could meet.

He picked her up, leaving her dress crumpled on the floor, and carried her over to the bed, where he flung her down and rid himself of his clothes. His naked body, as always, enthralled her. Her movements imbued with infinite sensuality, Celia took off her lacy black underwear, sliding her stockings down her legs, her eyes glittering with pagan invitation. Jethro said roughly, "I can't get enough of you."

For a moment, agony stabbed her to the heart. Sex, she thought. That's all he wants of me. Sex. Not love.

"What's wrong?" he said sharply.

She reached for him, pulling him on top of her, his weight crushing her into the bed. Then she kissed him with all her pent-up emotion, laving his lips with her tongue. He rolled over, pulling her with him, her hair tumbling over the pillow; and all the while their mouths were locked together in a kiss that neither asked for nor gave any quarter. Then Jethro raised his head, taking her breasts in his hands, watching all the changing expressions on her face with the total concentration that she knew so well and was helpless to resist.

Waves of feeling rippled through her. She threw back her head, moaning with pleasure, arching her hips against him. His fingers sought out the juncture of her thighs, so sleek and warm and ready. As she writhed beneath him, he thrust into her. She dug her nails into his shoulders, his back, frantic for him, beyond pride or restraint.

"Now, Jethro, now," she begged, and from a long way away remembered she'd said she wouldn't beg him for anything.

His powerful strokes, deeper and deeper, ignited every nerve in Celia's body. She felt her own throbbing and his as one, heard him cry out as he emptied within her, and surrendered herself to her own tumultuous release.

Then, very slowly, she came back to herself. To a man's skin slick with sweat, a man's face buried in her shoulder; his heart pounding against her rib cage. To intimacy without emotion and to the briefest of unions. A love-making that had never mentioned the word *love*.

Had they made love? Or had it been more primitive than that? Had it been yet another stage in the battle between her and Jethro? Perhaps, she thought, they'd made war, not love. There'd been no tenderness, no subtlety in that fierce coupling.

She lay very still and closed her eyes, knowing she couldn't bear to talk to him; there was nothing more to say. She forced her breathing to slow and deepen, her limbs to relax, and after a few minutes felt Jethro lift his weight from her. "Celia?" he whispered.

Her arm was lying across her face, her hair like a silken shield. She felt him cover her with the sheet; then he rolled over, away from her.

She waited in the darkness, not daring to move. She couldn't cry. This went too deep for tears.

She'd never felt such terrible loneliness as she did now, in bed beside the man she had married.

The man she loved.

CHAPTER THIRTEEN

WHEN Jethro woke, it was daylight. Automatically he turned over, seeking out the warmth of Celia's body; he'd already grown used to sharing his bed. Used to it? He craved it.

She wasn't there. Apart from him, the bed was empty. He glanced at his watch. Eight o'clock. It couldn't be. He never slept that late.

He was supposed to go to Atlanta today.

His body felt as though someone had pummeled him; as he stretched, he noticed the faint red marks of Celia's nails on his shoulder. He didn't remember her doing that. He didn't remember much about last night after he'd kissed her against the door. He'd totally lost control. Lost any vestige of technique or nuance. She'd been so upset with him, so furious that he'd deceived her once again; yet she'd made love to him with the ferocity of a wildcat.

Would he ever understand her?

He got out of bed. Her dress was still lying on the floor. He picked it up, catching her perfume from the fabric. He wanted her again, he thought, scowling, and headed for the bathroom.

On the marble counter was a folded note with his name on the outside. He stared at it, his muscles tensing. "Celia?" he called, and was answered only by silence.

She was probably down with her father.

Ellis rarely got up before ten. Where was she?

He opened the note.

My father thinks I'm going to Atlanta with you. I can't, Jethro. I've got to get away by myself and think. Please don't tell him I'm not with you, and please don't try and find me.

Celia

It was scribbled, as though she'd been in a hurry. He went through into her dressing room, and saw more evidence of a hurried departure. The flat box that had held his gift of the gold chain lay on top of her bureau, empty.

A chain. How symbolic of him, he thought. She'd used the word *trap*, hadn't she? Trapped in a loveless marriage. Chained to a man she hated.

Yet she'd taken the chain with her.

Or else she'd thrown it out the window. He wouldn't put that past her.

He had an ache in his gut as big as an oil tanker. Chain or no chain, she'd left him. Temporarily, no doubt, because of Ellis. But she was still gone, and he had no idea where.

As he went back through the bathroom, he caught sight of his naked body in the tall mirror. She didn't hate his body. He could still smell her scent on his skin; in his ears echoed her wild, impassioned cries of satiation.

He'd looked on her as a challenge, as a woman who never bored him, a woman he desired in ways that made nonsense of any words he could find to describe such a depth of need. But Celia was a challenge he'd failed.

She'd proved that by leaving him. She wasn't into manipulation. If she'd gone, their marriage was over. Contract or no contract.

It had never been a real marriage anyway.

He grabbed his razor and began to shave. There were ways he could find out where she'd gone. But he was damned if he was going to do that. If she wanted time to think, let her have it. He wasn't going to chase after her. Not his style.

He was better off without her.

A resolve that stayed with him all the way to the airport. His private jet was waiting for him out on the tarmac. His business in Atlanta was important. But as he edged through the crowds in the air-conditioned terminal, his briefcase in one hand, a single word was drumming through Jethro's brain. *Failure*.

Celia wasn't after his money. Never had been. And in a strange way he knew that had nothing to do with her father's fortune. If she'd been only a Coast Guard operator, she still wouldn't have chased him for his money.

In the brief time they'd been together, she'd shown him courage and honesty, passion and generosity. She'd laughed with him and cried in front of him. She was so beautiful it hurt him somewhere deep inside, in a place he'd never allowed a woman to reach him before.

He stopped near one of the ticket counters, taking her note out of his pocket, smoothing it and reading it once again. *Why did you marry me?* she'd asked him last night. He'd said something about her father, which had been true as far as it went. It just didn't go far enough. Basically, his marriage to Celia had very little to do with Ellis Scott.

The other reason he'd offered her—a less-than-flattering motive for marriage—was boredom. Boredom didn't go far enough either, even though Celia had jolted him out of a lifestyle that had become entirely too comfortable and predictable.

Why *had* he married her?

Did he really want the answer to that question?

A little boy banged into him, the mother apologized profusely and through it all Jethro stood like a man stunned. What if he'd fallen in love with Celia? Was that what he didn't want to admit? What he was avoiding like the plague?

He'd never been in love. He'd been too busy amassing his millions and then too cynical about women even to consider the possibility. But in a storm at sea he'd heard a woman's voice, and he'd followed that voice to a Newfoundland village where he'd found a chestnut-haired beauty who'd touched him to the core.

He didn't love her, of course he didn't. That was one challenge he wasn't ready for. Never would be. But in some deeply primitive way she was his, she was important to him. Too important for him to go off to Atlanta. He headed for the nearest bank of phones and started dialing. And an hour later, he was headed north for Vermont.

Celia, he'd found out, had bought a ticket to Burlington. She must be going to the lodge; on their honeymoon he'd recognized how much she liked his retreat. Gazing out the window of his jet at the White Mountains of New Hampshire, Jethro grimaced as he remembered that non-honeymoon. He'd been out to prove that he was in control; that he could spend the weekend with her and not devour her like a starving man.

Yeah, right. All he'd accomplished was to convince Celia he had a mistress tucked away in Manhattan. Smart move, Jethro. Real smart. And the only place he'd been remotely honest with her since then was in bed. There, his body had spoken a language he couldn't speak out loud.

No wonder she hated him. He'd deceived her about his money, about Michael Stansey and Ellis, about sex and about his feelings. As a result of which, she didn't think he had any.

He had plenty, he thought grimly. All of them coalesced into a hard lump in the pit of his stomach. Celia wouldn't be happy to be found. She wasn't playing games by running away. It was for real.

What was he going to say to her when he found her? You're important to me? Sure thing. That'd put him right up there with all the great romantics. His fleets of tankers, his corporations and his staff were important to him. How about, you've gotten under my skin? That was about as romantic as a dead porcupine.

He needed a scriptwriter, that's what he needed. Preferably one with a leaning toward poetry. With an impatient sigh, Jethro tried to focus on some of the papers in his briefcase. He'd figure out what he was going to say when he found her.

In Burlington, Celia had rented a car, a black Grand Am. So she must be headed for the lodge. But a couple of hours later, when he turned up the long driveway to his private retreat, Jethro was no nearer a solution as to how to deal with his errant wife. Maybe just seeing her again would tell him what to say.

It was a dull gray day, heavy clouds overhanging the hills, occasional gusts of rain driving against his windshield. The leaves were being whipped from the trees; it was cold. He turned the last corner and jammed on his brakes.

A black Grand Am was halfway in the ditch, the hood dented against the trunk of a spruce tree.

In two seconds Jethro was out of his own car. He yanked open the driver's door. Celia wasn't slumped down on the seat. She wasn't anywhere to be seen. No blood, he noticed, no cracks in the windshield. Through the roaring in his ears, he yelled, "Celia! Celia, it's Jethro."

Oak leaves rattled over his head; raindrops struck his

forehead like tiny bullets. Maybe she had concussion and had wandered off into the woods.

He'd check the lodge first.

He gunned his car up the driveway, gravel spitting from his tires. No lights on in the lodge, no signs of occupation and the front door locked tight. He walked through the empty rooms, calling her name even though he knew it was an exercise in futility. She hadn't been inside. He knew it in his bones.

Apart from anything else, she didn't have a key.

It would be dark early today and the temperature was supposed to drop substantially. He had to find her.

Because he loved her.

As if someone had hit him with a baseball bat, Jethro stood stock still. He loved her. It had taken a wrecked car, an empty house and grinding terror to show him the truth. A truth that had been staring him in the face ever since he'd heard her voice over the VHF radio.

He was in love with Celia. His wife.

He didn't know where she was.

He went up to the bedroom and changed into jeans and hiking boots, throwing on a rain-jacket over a heavy sweater. Then he forced himself to stop and think. The keys had been lying on the seat of the Grand Am; first he'd check to see if her bags were in the trunk. Then he'd call the Mortimers, the couple who looked after the lodge for him, and see if they'd heard from her; although he was almost certain he'd never told her their name.

And after that, Jethro?

He ran outside. It was raining hard now, sweeps of rain driven by the wind; his hair was soaked by the time he reached her car. But the trunk was empty. So she at least had some warm clothes with her. The Mortimers, he discovered, hadn't spoken to anyone but him all day, but they'd keep an eye out for her; fortunately, their New England reticence prevented them from asking any awkward questions.

If he'd been Celia, without transportation and with no key to the lodge, and with rain coming on, where would he have gone?

To the cabin, he thought in a surge of excitement. She wouldn't be afraid of heading up the mountain by herself, not Celia. He'd leave the front door unlocked and some lights on and get up there as quickly as he could. From his desk he took a piece of paper, scrawling on it where he'd gone in case she came back in his absence; at the bottom of the note, knowing it was a monumental step, he wrote, "I love you."

She didn't love him. She'd made that clear. So why was he telling her something she wouldn't want to hear?

It'd be her turn to laugh, he thought savagely. But he was through with deception. He'd done enough harm by keeping the truth from her. More than enough.

Behind him the front door opened.

He whirled, his heart thudding in his chest. Celia was standing in the doorway, staring at him as though she'd never seen him before. Her cheeks were white, her raingear dripping on the mat. She faltered, "It's raining."

She was shivering. Jethro's tongue seemed to be stuck to the roof of his mouth. With a huge effort, he said stupidly, "I was just writing you a note. Then I was going up to the cabin to look for you."

"I was partway there when it started to rain. So I decided I'd break a window in the lodge." Her smile was a mere movement of her lips. "But now that you're here, I don't have to do anything illegal. Just as well. We're a great pair for legalities, aren't we?"

Say something, Jethro. Or more to the point, do something. He crossed the room in three quick strides, pulled her into the room and closed the door. He could have said, "I love you." It was the logical time. Swiftly he decided he'd save it for when they were in bed, a fire in the hearth, the curtains drawn against the blackness of night. When their arms were around each other, her naked body close to his. A time when romance might have half a chance. "Your forehead's bruised," he said.

"I hit the windshield. A deer ran right across the driveway, that's how I wrecked the car."

Details, he thought; neither of them saying anything near the real truth. "You're cold. I'll start a fire and heat some soup."

"Okay," she said, avoiding his eyes.

When he came back from the big stone hearth, where flames were now crackling cheerily, she was standing by the kitchen counter, his note in her hand. She said in a hostile voice, "Did you write this?"

His heart felt like it was trying to bang its way out of his rib cage. "Yes," he said.

She pushed back her hood. Her hair shone in the light; her hand was trembling. "Don't play any more games with me, Jethro, I can't stand it. You don't love me."

He felt ten times more afraid than he had on *Starspray*. Or on the descent of K2, when a blizzard had struck, marooning them in a camp at 7,800 meters for two days with almost no food. "Yes, I do," he said, with as much emotion in his voice as if he were discussing a freighter's load capacity.

"You don't! You lust after me. You're not bored when I'm around. You might even like me—sometimes. But love—huh, not you."

"Celia," he said in a cracked voice, "I think I fell in love with you on *Starspray*. For sure I did outside the

Coast Guard depot that first morning. But I've been hiding the truth from myself as much as from you. I've never been in love in my life. No interest in it. Until you came along.''

''You came here to get me because you can't stand the prospect of being humiliated in front of my father.''

''That's not true! I came here because I had no choice.''

She pushed a wet strand of hair back from her face. ''Twice you've deceived me—how can I trust anything you say?''

''I didn't tell you I was rich because the amount of money I've got changes the way people behave around me—you know that from your own experience. What about Darryl? Did he want you or your money? I didn't tell you about Dr. Stansey...hell, it was because subconsciously I was afraid you wouldn't marry me if I did.'' He gripped the edge of the counter. ''How's that for honesty?''

She was backed against the refrigerator as though he were an enemy. He added with all the force of his personality, ''Look, I know you don't love me. You've never pretended to and God knows I've given you precious little reason to. But I had to tell you the truth!''

In an unreadable voice, she said, ''So our marriage isn't just about sex?''

''I'd be a liar if I didn't say your body drives me out of my mind...but it's *your* body, Celia. Inseparable from the rest of you. Dammit, I don't even know the words.''

He had no clue what she was thinking. *Go for broke, Jethro*, he told himself, and added hoarsely, ''I can't live without you. It's that simple.''

She was shivering again, although twin patches of hectic color were staining her cheekbones. In swift compunction, he said, ''I should have saved all this heavy-duty emotion for later instead of dumping it all over you. Why don't you have a hot bath? And I'll put some soup on…we can eat in front of the fire.'' With a humility new to him, he finished, ''Then, if you want to, we could go to bed. Maybe there I can show you I love you. With my body. I'm not so hot on words—that's something I've learned since I woke up this morning and found you gone.''

''You're doing just fine,'' Celia said.

She had straightened, standing tall. Her eyes, he saw with the first glimmer of hope, were shining; they looked as though she'd just made love. ''It was never just sex,'' he said evenly. ''I know I said it was, but I was lying. Lying to myself more than to you. Bed was the one place I could tell you the truth. Let my feelings out. Because I've got feelings, Celia, don't ever doubt that.''

''I don't—''

She was going to tell him she didn't love him. ''You don't have to say anything,'' he interrupted. ''Except whether you'd prefer carrot soup or minestrone. You're cold and tired and I'm a jerk to keep you—''

''Jethro,'' Celia said, ''shut up.''

''Come back to Washington with me,'' he said forcibly. ''That's all I ask. Give us a chance. I swear I won't deceive you again. Ever.''

''You mean we can't stay the night here?'' she said with a levity that didn't quite come off. Then she walked over to him, clasped the front of his wet rain-jacket, and kissed him full on the mouth. Her lips were cold. With a huge effort he kept his hands at his sides, his body immobile.

She stepped back, and for a moment panic flared in her face. ''I—you do still want me, don't you?''

"Want you? I always do, I always will. But first I have to know if you believe me. If we've got a chance together."

Very deliberately she unzipped her jacket, fumbled at the neckline of her shirt and drew out the gold chain, the sapphire twinkling against the back of her hand. "I couldn't bear to take this off," she said. "You gave it to me as a wedding present, you're the one who put it round my neck."

Delicacy and strength. "What are you getting at?"

"Oh Jethro, don't you see? I love you, too."

He swallowed hard. "I—would you mind repeating that?"

"I love you. I love you. I love you." She laughed, a sudden cascade of sound. "Shall I keep going? I can if you want me to."

"You mean it?" he said blankly.

"I keep telling you I'm a lousy liar."

"That necklace—I was so afraid I'd chained you, trapped you in a marriage you didn't want."

Tears were shining in her eyes more brightly than the diamonds on her necklace. "I want it. If you do."

She meant it. She loved him, wanted to be married to him. He swept her up into his arms, wet rain-jacket and all. "Come to bed with me, my darling. Now."

"In front of the fire," she said with endearing shyness. "On the carpet. Like the first time we made love."

"That morning in the attic." His smile faded. "Part of the reason I didn't touch you on our honeymoon was to prove—to myself as much as to you—that I was in control. But underneath, I was running scared. Scared I'd find out how much you meant to me. So all weekend I treated you like a stick of furniture."

"You've been given a second chance," Celia said. "I'm cold, Jethro. Warm me...please?"

A second chance. His heart thudding against his ribs, Jethro took off her jacket and sweater, easing her rainpants and slacks down her legs. Then he took a couple of pillows from the chesterfield and threw them on the rug. As she sank to the floor, the firelight danced over her face. "I love you, Celia," he said huskily. "More than I can say."

"Then show me," she said, and opened her arms to him.

As he peeled off his shirt, he said, "I can't ask you to marry me because we already are. But the words we said that day...to love and to cherish until death do us part...that's my promise to you."

Two tears spilled to her cheeks. "And mine to you."

For a moment, wordlessly, he held her close. He held the world in his arms, he thought. Because she was his world.

They made love slowly and with infinite tenderness, although as always it ended in a tumult of release. As Jethro raised his head, gazing into his wife's face, he said unsteadily, "You took me to a place I've never been before—because we love each other and that changes everything."

"Sweetheart..." Celia said.

He followed the curve of her collarbone with his fingertip. "You asked me once not to call you that."

"I've always wanted to keep it for the man I love, who loves me. That's you, Jethro, don't you see?"

He felt ten feet tall and incredibly humble both at the same time. With a lightness that didn't quite work, he said, "You mean we can do without honey?"

"And don't you ever call me baby."

"Maybe we need a new contract," Jethro teased.

"No way! In fact, let's tear up that awful document Mr. Wilkins drew up. I hated it from the start."

In sudden urgency, he said, "I know I've been close-mouthed about my childhood, my mother and father. But I can tell you anything, can't I? About keeping Lindy away from my dad when he was drinking. About Dave encouraging me after Dad died, because he had faith in me and knew I could get the business back on its feet. About how lonely I was after my mother left even though I'm not sure she ever really loved Lindy and me...." He kissed the exquisite line of Celia's cheekbone, where the flames cast a glow on her skin. "I can tell you anything. Although I can still hardly believe that you love me."

She turned in his arms, cuddling to his chest. "You're stuck with me, Jethro."

He laughed. "We're not stuck with making love on the carpet for the rest of our days, are we?"

"Nope. The bed will be fine next time." Gently she nibbled at his lower lip. "This is our real honeymoon."

Jethro stroked her bare breast with lingering pleasure. "Can't get much more real than this."

She gave a sigh of pure happiness. "We could stay a couple of days, couldn't we? I could phone my dad so he wouldn't worry."

With no finesse whatsoever, Jethro said, "Would you like to have children?"

"Oh yes," she said warmly, "your children."

"Then you'd better ask your dad how he feels about grandchildren."

"The wonderful thing is, it looks like he'll be around when they're born," she whispered. "I've got you to thank for that, Jethro."

"Me and Michael Stansey. How many children, Celia?"

"Two," she said dreamily. "We can teach them how to fly and sail and climb mountains."

"We can tell them we love them," Jethro said roughly.

"You never had that, did you?" she said in quick distress.

He moved his bare shoulders restlessly. "No...but I'm learning fast. From you."

"Our children will have two parents who love each other and them," she said fiercely.

Celia would never abandon her children. Not like his mother, he thought with a catch in his throat. "Dave could be their godfather."

"We're kind of planning ahead here," she said demurely.

He laughed. "Talking of planning ahead, how about that soup? All I had for breakfast was a coffee at the airport."

She ran her tongue down his breastbone. "Minestrone and you. That's a menu it's hard to beat."

With overt sensuality Jethro kissed the sweet slope of her breast. "You're dessert," he said. "A lot tastier than chocolate cream pie from the Seaview Grill."

One thing led to another; it was quite some time before Jethro put the minestrone in the microwave.

Getting down
to business in
the boardroom...
and the bedroom!

A secret romance, a forbidden affair,
a thrilling attraction...

What happens when two people work
together and simply can't help falling in
love—no matter how hard they try to resist?

Find out in our new series of stories set
against working backgrounds.

Look out for

THE MISTRESS CONTRACT
by Helen Brooks, Harlequin Presents® #2153
Available January 2001

and don't miss

SEDUCED BY THE BOSS
by Sharon Kendrick, Harlequin Presents® #2173
Available April 2001

Available wherever Harlequin books are sold.

HARLEQUIN®
Makes any time special ™

Visit us at www.eHarlequin.com

HP925

He's a man of cool sophistication.
He's got pride, power and wealth.
He's a ruthless businessman, an expert lover—
and he's one hundred percent committed
to staying single.

Until now. Because suddenly he's responsible
for a BABY!

HIS BABY

An exciting miniseries from Harlequin Presents®
He's sexy, he's successful...
and now he's facing up to fatherhood!

On sale February 2001:
RAFAEL'S LOVE-CHILD
by Kate Walker, Harlequin Presents® #2160

On sale May 2001:
MORGAN'S SECRET SON
by Sara Wood, Harlequin Presents® #2180

And look out for more later in the year!

Available wherever Harlequin books are sold.

HARLEQUIN®
Makes any time special ™

Visit us at www.eHarlequin.com   HPBABY

INDULGE IN A QUIET MOMENT
WITH HARLEQUIN

Get a FREE
Quiet Moments
Bath Spa

with just two proofs of purchase from
any of our four special collector's editions in May.

Harlequin® is sure to make your time special this Mother's Day
with four special collector's editions featuring a short story
PLUS a complete novel packaged together in one volume!

Collection #1 Intrigue abounds in a collection featuring *New York Times* bestselling author Barbara Delinsky and Kelsey Roberts.

Collection #2 Relationships? Weddings? Children? = *New York Times* bestselling author Debbie Macomber and Tara Taylor Quinn at their best!

Collection #3 Escape to the past with *New York Times* bestselling author Heather Graham and Gayle Wilson.

Collection #4 Go West! With *New York Times* bestselling author Joan Johnston and Vicki Lewis Thompson!

Plus Special Consumer Campaign!

Each of these four collector's editions will feature a
"FREE QUIET MOMENTS BATH SPA" offer.
See inside book in May for details.

Only from

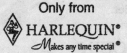

HARLEQUIN®
Makes any time special ®

Don't miss out! Look for this exciting promotion on sale in May 2001,
at your favorite retail outlet.